MURDER IN AN EDINBURGH PARK

DI MCKENZIE BOOK 4

ANNA-MARIE MORGAN

For Jean and Christopher, with love.

ALSO BY ANNA-MARIE MORGAN

The DI McKenzie Series (4 books so far)

Book 1 - Murder on Arthur's Seat

Book 2 - Murder at Greyfriars Kirk

Book 3 - Murder in the Bookkeeper's Attic

Book 4 - Murder in an Edinburgh Park

The DI Giles Series (23 books so far)

Book 1 - Death Master

Book 2 - You Will Die

Book 3 - Total Wipeout

Book 4 - Deep Cut

Book 5 - The Pusher

Book 6 - Gone

Book 7 - Bone Dancer

Book 8 - Blood Lost

Book 9 - Angel of Death

Book 10 - Death in the Air

Book 11 - Death in the Mist

Book 12 - Death under Hypnosis

Book 13 - Fatal Turn

Book 14 - The Edinburgh Murders

Book 15 - A Picture of Murder

Book 16 - The Wilderness Murders

Book 17 - The Bunker Murders

Book 18 - The Garthmyl Murders

Book 19 - The Signature

Book 20 - The Incendiary Murders

Book 21 - The Park Murders

Book 22 - The Powys Murders

Book 23 - The Backstreet Murders

Copyright © 2024 by Anna-marie Morgan

All rights reserved.

No part of this book may be reproduced in any form or by any electronic or mechanical means, including information storage and retrieval systems, without written permission from the author, except for the use of brief quotations in a book review.

This work is a work of fiction.

PROLOGUE

Caitlin Murray dipped a hand into her bag and pulled out a single colour photograph, fingers lingering on its worn edges, before handing it to her friend, Isla Campbell. "Will you keep this somewhere safe for me? I'll let you know when I need it back."

Isla took the image, feeling its curled corners under her fingertips. She turned it the right way up to see it properly. A single, striking oak tree stood proudly atop a hill, its lower branches spread like a parasol, shading the ground below. Sunlight streamed through the leaves, creating dappled patterns on the grass.

"Lovely photo," she murmured, tilting her head, trying to place the location. "You met someone on one of your little trips, eh?" She grinned, showing perfectly even chalk-white teeth.

Caitlin's lips curved in a smile, but it didn't reach her eyes. Instead, her gaze drifted past her friend, as though searching for something, or someone. "Don't lose it," she said, her voice quiet, but firm.

Isla frowned, sensing the shift in the other woman's mood.

"Cait, what's this about? It's not like you to be mysterious with me. This tree... why is it important?"

Caitlin hesitated, fingers tapping the edge of her bag, before she folded her hands together. "It's... just a photo. I need to know it's safe, that's all."

"Right." Isla's light tone disguising the confusion she felt as she slipped the photograph into a pocket inside of her handbag. "Consider it in safekeeping. Though I'd love to know the reason you've given it to me."

"All will become clear, eventually, I'm sure." Caitlin answered. There was an edge to her tone, surprising them both. She exhaled, softening it. "Just... trust me, Isla. If I ask for it back, don't ask questions. Just give it to me, please?"

Isla blinked, a ripple of unease spreading through her. "Sure, Cait. Whatever you want." She closed her handbag's clasp. "It's as good as locked in a vault."

Her friend smiled, the muscles in her face relaxing, but the glazed look in her eyes didn't fade. "Thanks," she murmured, before glancing at her watch. "I've got to run."

"Sure, but..." Isla called as her friend turned to leave, "you'd tell me if something was wrong, wouldn't you?"

Caitlin paused in the doorway, silhouetted in the afternoon sun. She turned her head enough for Isla to catch the flicker of something unspoken in her expression. Then, with a nod goodbye, she walked away, leaving the question hanging unanswered in the air.

Isla watched her go, her handbag feeling somehow heavier with the photograph inside. Not from the weight of it, but the mysterious air with which it had been given.

∼

1

DEATH AT DAWN

Thirty-two-year-old Caitlin Murray checked her watch. Four minutes past seven. Plenty of time for her run to the Scott Tower before starting work.

She tied her laces, tightened her ponytail, slipped in ear buds, and adjusted her head torch. After turning up the volume on her phone, the young woman zipped it up in her bum bag. The fitness tracker confirmed a heart rate of sixty-four beats per minute, as she began the intended six-mile run from Orchard Brae Avenue in Craigleith, along Queensferry and Hillhouse Road, and then a left turn up through the Corstophine Woods and back.

Although December had started with frigid bite, two weeks in and the weather had mellowed to a familiar dreich with a monotonous grey sky. Perhaps there would be snow before Christmas, but she wouldn't hold her breath. It felt too warm for it.

One-hundred-and-twenty-seven beats per minute, and she was in full flow; breathing hard but regular as she rose above the western suburbs of Edinburgh, through one of the city's largest parks.

Listening to her favourite Billie Eilish song, she heard little else. Not even the slap of her trainers as they impacted muddy surface water on a trail sided by that autumn's rotting leaves. Passing moss-caked trees, she reached the rocky path to the top, where gorse, grasses, and bare trees dominated. Caitlin checked her tracker. Elevation gain, three-hundred-and-ninety-three feet. She could see the city lights below, and could just make out the snow-topped mountains beyond. Sometimes she paused at this spot to take it all in. But not today. Today she wanted to get to work early. No stopping this morning. Not until she reached the tower.

As she approached the Walter Scott memorial through the trees, with its buttressed corners and crenellated parapet, she passed the outer fencing of the famous Edinburgh Zoo. But there were no animals near today. Shame. She enjoyed catching the odd glimpse.

She stopped next to the tower, bending over to catch her breath, music murmuring in her ears. It was still dark, and not a soul about. Caitlin was alone at the tower, or so she thought.

The first blow to her head knocked her sideways. Blood pulsated in her ears. Vision blurred. Everything slowed. Time stretched. A stumble. A voice. Another blow. Knees failed. The lights went out.

GRANT MCKENZIE LEANED back against his car, waving goodbye to his youngest children, Martha and Craig. His eldest, Davie, now aged eleven, took the bus. Jane, the DI's wife, would usually handle the school run. But she had a hospital appointment at the Western General this morning, so her husband was doing the honours, meaning a late start for him at the station. He lingered for a moment, staring at the backs of his children as they lolloped with their bags towards the entrance, in case they turned to wave again, and hoping they would have a good day. His phone buzzed in his pocket.

"McKenzie..."

"Grant?" It was DS Susan Robertson. "Are you on your way?"

"Aye." He checked his watch. "I'll be there in around twenty-five minutes."

"Can you meet me at Corstophine Tower?"

He frowned. "Corstophine Tower?"

"They discovered a woman bludgeoned to death this morning. I'm on my way up there. I thought you would probably want to see the crime scene for yourself, and it's easier for you to go straight there."

"That's true." He unlocked his car, pulling open the driver's door. "I'll be with you as soon as I can."

ON APPROACHING the tower along the wooded, muddy trail, McKenzie could see the tent erected over the victim's body between two bare trees. Number markers lay strewn around, highlighting blood traces and dropped belongings. "Was it an attempted robbery gone wrong?" he asked, on approaching Susan, who was in discussion with a constable positioned a few feet from the tent.

Behind them, the tower loomed, a silent witness to the horror which had befallen the young woman.

The DS shook her head. "We don't know. She was wearing a bag around her waist. The killer presumably tipped its contents onto the ground after he attacked her. The victim's phone was still playing music when officers arrived."

He frowned. "She'd not been dead long then?"

"We'll suit up, and we can have a good look at her. A runner found her shortly after six this morning. He said it seemed like someone had attacked her not long before. The guy who found her has given a statement, and will be in to speak with us later today. He saw her feet first. They were sticking out towards the trail. He's pretty shaken up by the whole thing. He's taken the day off work."

Grant cast his eyes over the bloodied trail through the grass. "I'm not surprised. Let's see for her ourselves."

After donning forensic suits and overshoes, they entered the small marquee where the bloodied victim lay in a heap, still clothed in jogging gear.

"It doesn't look like the killer sexually assaulted her. But he made a helluva mess of her head."

Susan nodded.

The forensic officer made room for them to fully view the body. "He hit her several times with something heavy."

"Have they found the murder weapon?"

"Not yet, but the search is due to start any moment. A team of officers are on their way. We've got a wide cordon in place. The trail is closed for the foreseeable."

"Aye, good." McKenzie rose. "So they smashed in her skull and dragged her to the side. It wasn't a proper attempt to hide the body, though, was it? Why bother dragging her at all if there was no intention to interfere with her."

"Unless he dressed her again afterwards."

"Aye well, Fiona can tell us whether that happened." Grant sighed. "But if it wasn't for sexual reasons, and the killer didn't rob her, why the attack? It must be personal. Do we know who she is?"

"Not yet, sir. But we expect to know soon."

"If she's got a husband or boyfriend, I want to speak to them as soon as. This was more than a murder. It looks like overkill to me."

Susan stepped back, allowing the forensic officer space to get back to work. "Maybe something disturbed the killer. He may have intended moving the body further away from the trail, but heard someone coming, and legged it."

"We'll need CCTV from all the cameras in the area. We need to know which way she came into the park, and whether anyone followed her."

"Graham and Helen are chasing that up for us, sir. Maybe the perp lay in wait for her up here. This may have been her daily route."

"Could be... Let's find out who she is, and we can take it from there."

Before going back to the car, McKenzie looked around. The day was damp, but not cold. Mud on the trail was soft. There would be a good many footprints, likely including the perpetrator's. Off in the distance, he could hear the city's traffic. Likely, the victim would have been at work or on her way by now if she hadn't run into her killer. As he made his way back to the vehicle, he cast his eyes around, wondering if the murderer was watching. He fastened his long coat, feeling visceral anger towards the cowardly dog who had taken the woman's life. The sooner he was behind bars, the better.

2

A LIFE FULL OF PROMISE

Graham Dalgleish put down the phone as Grant and Susan walked in. "Got a name for you. The victim was a thirty-two-year-old living in Craigleith. Caitlin Murray. Business woman, apparently, but that's all I have at the moment."

McKenzie threw his coat on a peg. "How did you get the identity so fast?"

"The runner who found her, name of Danny Ross, said he had seen her many times on the trail. Ross runs it regularly, and said he thinks Caitlin ran it most days when she was in the country."

"In the country? Did she travel a lot, then?"

"Aye, seems like it."

"Well, find out everything you can about Caitlin, and I would like to speak to Danny Ross. He seems to know a bit about her. I would like to hear the story from his lips and take a look at the man for myself."

"I'll arrange it." Dalgleish nodded.

"Also, we need addresses and details of any partners and ex-partners for Caitlin. And get a good look at her home."

"On it, sir."

"We've requested copies of CCTV footage from cameras in the area," Helen McAllister approached from her desk. "We should have them by this afternoon."

"Good." Grant nodded. "I'll collate what we have and get it on the board. We need to know everything about this woman, right down to her shoe size. I have a feeling her murder was personal. I think her killer hated her. The question is, why?"

Dr Fiona Campbell donned latex gloves as she and McKenzie regarded the victim lying on the cold stainless steel surface.

"It looks to me like overkill. He hit her more times than was necessary to kill her." The DI stepped back, giving the pathologist room, noting the shadows under her eyes. He could tell she was tired, but she approached the victim in the same professional manner she always did.

She turned the victim's head, probing it with gentle fingers. "We'll get some x-rays, but it's obvious her skull has several fractures. Most of the bleeding was from these head wounds. The perp wasn't messing about. He knew these blows would kill her."

"Would you agree it was overkill?"

She contemplated it. "I don't know if I'd go that far. But he certainly intended ending her life. And it was more than one blow. Two or three, maybe? Using something heavy... There's no obvious puncture wound, so large, bulky, and blunt. A rock, maybe? Did you find the murder weapon?"

"Not yet. The search is ongoing."

"It could be overkill, but I think it is more likely the killer was simply making certain she was dead."

Dr Campbell began her examination of the rest of the body. "Aside from a bruise to her upper left arm and hip, there appear to be no injuries to the rest of the body. Likely, the bruises resulted from impacting the ground when she fell. Mud stained her clothing on the left side and covered her left leg. She fell that way after being hit on the right side of her head. She didn't die straight away. There's mud caked in her left palm. She was probably trying to get up by pushing with that hand."

"Did she fight back?"

"I doubt she'd have had the strength after the first blow, and there is no bruising or swelling of the hands. But we've taken scrapings from under the nails to look for perpetrator DNA. And her clothes and vaginal swaps are also being examined for DNA, fibres, etcetera. From what we can see, there was no evidence of sexual assault, and the only clothes they found were on her body. She had on black lycra running shorts, a vest top, and a sports hoodie. Plus underwear. Her socks and trainers were also still on her feet. The was so much blood around her head, it took me a few moments to realise she was blonde."

"And you say the killer approached her from the right."

"He hit her on the right side of her head, yes. And, I suspect, as she tried to get up, he hit her again."

"So either the assailant is lefthanded, or they approached her from behind or from the right."

"That's how it appears, yes."

"She was a businesswoman, apparently. An entrepreneur with a bright future ahead of her."

Fiona nodded. "I had heard the name before."

"Had you?" Grant raised both brows.

"There was a magazine piece on her not that long ago. Caitlin Murray was out in Colombia, sourcing beans from high in the mountains. Her brand promised quality and goodness. I tried some of her coffee in a shop on Cockburn Street. If I remember rightly, it was excellent. There was a chalk-board above the counter, highlighting the latest award-winning beans."

"And I hadn't heard of her." McKenzie shook his head. "I really ought to get out more."

"She was still up and coming. Although, according to the article, she had been running the company for several years. The company had been her dream since she was a teenager. I think she studied business at the university here in Edinburgh. The magazine might still be at home. I'll dig it out for you, if you like?"

"That would be very useful, Fiona. Thank you."

As Grant made his way back to the station, he thought about the young woman and the killer who had ruthlessly cut short her hopes and dreams. Perhaps the murderer was a business rival, though he doubted that. He couldn't imagine any of the baristas in Edinburgh taking someone's life over coffee beans. Still, stranger things had happened. If he was going to find the killer, he needed to know everything he could about Caitlin Murray.

3

THE MYSTERY AFTERSHAVE

Twenty-eight-year-old Danny Ross attended the station that afternoon to go over his statement with the DI and Susan Robertson. He looked nervously around as Grant led him to the interview room, and the DI noted sweat on the younger man's upper lip.

"Please, take a seat, Daniel." McKenzie pulled a chair back from the table for him.

Danny's hair appeared damp, suggesting he had showered before coming in. He stood around five feet eleven and had a lean but muscular frame. "Thank you," he said, as he sat.

Susan nodded her greeting to the red-haired runner.

"It must have given you quite the fright yesterday, eh?" The DI seated himself opposite Ross.

"Aye, it did. You don't expect to find that when you go for a run in the morning. And she seemed a nice lass, too."

"I understand you had spoken to her previously?"

"I had... a few times, actually. Mostly, it was just to wave hello when we saw each other on the trail. But, occasionally, if we bumped into each other at the top, we'd take a breather together. Chat about the weather."

"Ever chat about anything else?"

He shrugged, scratching his stubbled chin. "Maybe... work, I think? Nothing too personal."

"What do you do, Danny?" McKenzie leaned back in his chair.

"I work on cars." He held up his hands, showing them the ingrained engine oil in the grooves of his skin, and under his nails.

"You're a mechanic?"

"Aye, I work at a garage near Corstophine. I gave my details to the officer. Work and home."

"So, Danny, tell us what happened yesterday."

"When I found Miss Murray?"

"From the beginning of your day."

"From the beginning?" Ross frowned. "Why?"

"It helps your memory when you go through things sequentially. Helps you remember details."

"Oh, I see." He thought for a moment. "Well, I got up with the alarm at seven and got ready to go running. I washed, brushed my teeth and had a bowl of cereal and a banana. I live in Craigleith, so I usually go for a run, and then have a shower and some toast before going into the garage. Work usually starts before eight-thirty. And I find the run helps wake me up and gets me motivated."

"What time did you start your run?"

"Around seven-thirty."

"Have you always run?"

"Aye... Since I was a bairn. My ma said I was born running."

"So, you woke, ate cereal, and headed up Corstophine Woods."

"I run the same route every day because I like routine. I change my routes on weekends, but the Corstophine trail suits me during the week."

"Okay... Do you drive or run to the trail?"

"I run all the way from home, along the Queensferry Road."

"Did you notice anything unusual on the approach to the park?"

"No, I didn't."

"Did you see anyone hanging around or running away from the trail?"

"No."

"Did you speak to anyone on the way up through the woods?"

"I didn't see anyone. Not until I was running back towards home after calling police and giving my statement to officers when they arrived. I was really late to work yesterday. They told me to take today off because of the shock I was in. I think my hands shook all day. I lost count of the number of times I dropped a spanner before they told me to go home. You don't realise how things are going to affect you until you go through them. I thought I'd be okay to go back to work, but obviously I wasn't. It fair hit me hard, I'll tell you."

"Who did you see when you were on the way home?"

"No one in particular. I mean, I saw cars going along the road; people making their way to work, and a few dog walkers. I didn't see anyone suspicious or anything. But maybe I wasn't paying enough attention."

"So tell us what was happening just before you saw the body, and then what you saw as you approached the tower."

"Right, well, I was running up the trail. I remember it had been raining, and the paths were wet. It was still dark, but the sky was lightening. I had my headlamp on, though. This time of year, you need it. Running trails can be dangerous in the dark. Er, so I remember approaching the tower, and something white caught my eye on the ground. It was reflecting my headlamp. As I looked, I could see it was a white trainer with a reflective tick on it."

"A Nike shoe."

"Aye... Well, I stopped in my tracks. I jumped out of my skin when I saw a leg. I thought, at first, someone had fallen and was unconscious. But when I knelt next to the body, I realised it was Caitlin, and that she wasn't responding. I saw her hair looked matted and, when I tapped her cheek, I got blood on my hands. She was still warm, and I jumped back in shock. I realized that someone had murdered her, and I was terrified that the attacker might still be nearby, or that you guys might suspect it was me after I tried to revive her. I had her blood on me, after all. So, I telephoned police right away, and they told me officers would be there within minutes. The operator asked me questions about the woman, but my mind was spinning, and I stumbled over my words something awful. I'd never seen a dead body before. And I knew the woman. Those few minutes I waited were the longest of my life, I can tell you. I was shaking, expecting someone to jump out of the dark at me. Luckily, by then, it was getting lighter, though the sun was not yet up. Then the officers arrived and began questioning me and the ambulance staff went to the girl."

"Is this your statement?" Grant pushed the sheet towards Ross.

"Aye."

"Could you read it and confirm for me it is an accurate reflection of what occurred?"

Danny bent his head as he pored over the lines. "That's pretty much how it happened, yes."

"And you didn't see anyone up at the tower? Or running away?"

"No. They must have left before I got there."

"These times are tight." Grant steepled his hands as he surveyed the young man's face. "We have Caitlin on CCTV entering the park at seven-twenty. You enter at seven-thirty-five, and must have started your run from home before seven-thirty. You said you began it at seven-thirty."

"Aye well, maybe it was seven-fifteen or seven-twenty. I didn't check my watch until I entered the trail."

"And what time was that?"

"seven-thirty-five, like you said."

"Someone must have murdered Caitlin right before you arrived at the tower. Or within ten or fifteen minutes of your arrival."

"They must have done." Ross fell silent. His gaze dropped to the table. "It's a sobering thought, that. Maybe if I had got there sooner, I would be dead too."

"Or she would still be alive..." Grant lingered the words. "When did you wash the blood off?"

"Sorry?"

"Your hands... When did you wash them?"

"When I got home. I called my boss after I had given my statement and then went home and showered. I got into work about eleven. They could see I was in a state, and they told me to take today off. They thought I was suffering from delayed shock, but I think I my shock started when I found her, when I saw and felt the injuries, and the blood."

"You say you liked Caitlin?"

"Aye, she was a nice person. She seemed happy to me."

"How much did you know about her? What did you talk about?"

"Well, now you ask, I don't know that I knew much at all, really. I knew her name, and I knew she liked to run before work. I knew she was into coffee in a big way — buying beans and stuff. That's it, really. It's not much, is it?"

"Did you fancy her?"

"Eh?"

"Do you have a girlfriend?"

"I do. Her name is Elaine. She's all the woman I need. I didn't fancy Caitlin. She just seemed a gracious lady. A fellow early-bird. That's all."

"Did she fancy you?"

"If she did, she didn't say."

"Is there anything else you want to tell us, Danny?" Susan asked.

He shook his head.

"Very well." McKenzie rose from his seat. "I'll show you out. I want you to get in touch if you remember anything else."

"Okay." Ross zipped up his jacket. "I hope you catch him...whoever did this. Do you think he'll strike again? Hurt someone else on the trail?"

"We'll have officers posted around there for a while when it reopens."

"Phew. That's reassuring." Danny followed the DI down the corridor. "I didn't run this morning. I didn't feel safe."

CAITLIN MURRAY'S flat in Orchard Brae was almost exactly as Grant imagined it would be. The reception room, with off-white walls, was open-plan with the kitchen and diner, and was spacious and modern; filled with light and every expected convenience. It was so perfectly and precisely decorated, he could have been in an expensive hotel. Lit via down-lighters and copious windows, it had a calming effect on him. Its designer had tastefully presented the large bedrooms with white walls and accessories in muted colours, and decorated the two bathrooms with travertine tiles and bronze fixtures and fittings.

"Why did she live so lightly?" Grant asked Susan as he perused the almost empty granite worktops in the kitchen. "I mean, she didn't leave things lying around like most folks would." He opened the dishwasher. A single used bowl and glass lay on the top tray.

"Caitlin made her bed, but her walk-in wardrobe is a mess," Susan answered, "and some drawers in the home office are half open. Seems at odds with the rest of her home. But I agree, this place looks like a hotel. Like she didn't spend much time here."

"Aye well, she travelled a lot for her business, sourcing products abroad. I guess home was wherever she dropped her hat... or her bag."

"Looks like the second bedroom was her home-office," Susan called.

Grant followed her into the room where an open laptop sat on a desk near the window, along with an array of paperwork, some of which had fallen to the floor. Built-in shelving housed books, files, and contemporary art pieces. And two chests of drawers stood against the remaining walls, there being no bed in the room.

As Susan had said, someone had left drawers open. Grant thought he caught a faint whiff of something. A scent. Not perfume. Aftershave. Something woody. He couldn't put a name to it, though. "Do we know if she had a boyfriend?" He asked Susan.

"Helen was looking into that. She said Caitlin wasn't seeing anyone, currently. She split with her boyfriend eight months ago. Helen is asking him in for questioning."

"Good." McKenzie walked over to the chest, whose drawers were hanging out. "We should speak with friends and family, too."

The top drawer contained notebooks and a diary, brochures for Caitlin's coffee beans, and pens. The DI separated them so they could bag and tag them later, before leaving the home office for Caitlin's bedroom.

The victim had made her bed before setting off on her run, but, as Susan had pointed out, the wardrobe was in disarray. He smelled it again, the aftershave. Someone had been in here recently. Probably male. But what was he doing in a woman's wardrobe? Had someone been here before them? Looking for something? He surveyed the clothing on a long rail in front of him; the garments organised according to size and type. On the floor below were several items which appeared to have fallen from their hangers. Were they dirty? He didn't think so. When he picked them up, they still smelled strongly of fabric conditioner — one of his wife Jane's favourite brands. So why were they on the floor?

"Someone's been in here," he called to DS Robertson. "And recently. A man, I think."

"Really?" She appeared outside of the wardrobe's sliding doors. "What makes you say that?"

Grant stepped aside. "Go in and sniff the air."

She did as she was told, taking several inhalations, her nose twitching. "Ralph Loren, Polo Red."

"What?"

"The aftershave. It's Ralph Loren."

"Got you."

"And, you're right. I think someone came in here wearing it recently. But, with the wardrobe doors closed, the scent could have lingered for a while. A week, maybe more."

"I caught the same scent in the bedroom." He pressed his lips together.

"You think she slept with someone the night before she was murdered?"

"Maybe."

"Have you checked the bedsheets?"

He grimaced. "I am not sniffing bedsheets."

Susan laughed. "What kind of detective are you?"

"All right, I'll-"

"I'll do it." Susan grinned. "My nose is pretty good."

She disappeared, returning a minute later. "I can't smell aftershave on the sheets at all. Whoever he was, she didn't go to bed with him. He could have been a visitor, maybe?"

"Aye, maybe, but one who went through her drawers and wardrobe for whatever reason. That would be an odd sort of visitor."

"Looking for something?"

"That's what I'm thinking."

"The killer, perhaps?"

"Aye, maybe."

"I wonder what he was looking for?"

The DI perused the clothes and shelving down the side. "I'll do a thorough search. Maybe whoever it was didn't find what they were looking for."

"I'll leave you to it," Susan answered. "I'll check the bathroom and kitchen."

McKenzie began by checking the inner and outer pockets of jackets. Finding nothing, he searched the garments hanging up, followed by those folded and stacked on the shelving unit to the right-hand side of the rail, and then behind and to the back of the shelves. Nothing. He kneeled on the floor, going through Caitlin's shoes, and feeling a little odd at completing this further intrusion into the victim's personal things. Knees clicking, he stood up once satisfied nothing was there. Whoever had entered the victim's wardrobe had either found what they were looking for, or left disappointed. Grant had found nothing out of the ordinary.

As he turned to walk back into the bedroom, DS Robertson poked her head around the bedroom door. "Bingo," she said, holding up a handful of passports in gloved hands. "I found these held together with an elastic band in an empty tampon box."

"Old ones?" McKenzie frowned.

Susan shook her head. "Passports under various names." She opened them one by one. "Diane Murdoch, Ellie Maitland, Frances Ross, Sheila Rowat, and Carolyn MacIntosh. Here, look."

Grant checked the photographs. They were all the same woman when you looked hard enough, but she had changed the style and colour of her hair for each. She had used the passports at various times over the previous six years. Checking the stamps inside, it was clear Caitlin had been to several countries in South America, and on the continent. What was also clear was these trips were not for sourcing coffee beans. She wouldn't have needed a false identity to buy coffee. So what had she been doing?

"Looks like our Caitlin Murray may have been up to no good." Susan grimaced. "That'll make finding her killer that much harder, eh?"

"Maybe the people she worked with, or her ex-boyfriend, will know why she did all this." Grant took out an evidence bag. "We'll tag them and the box you found them in. Where was it, anyway?" he asked.

"Next to the clean towels in the bathroom alcove."

"Hidden in plain sight?"

"Aye... Any boyfriend would be unlikely to go looking in a tampon box."

"Right enough." He grimaced. "It's not something I've ever done."

"No, there's more to this victim than we imagined. I'll find out what I can about these trips." Susan handed McKenzie the passports. "Are we done here?"

"I reckon so. Crime scene officers may give it a once over. I'll let them know we think someone was in here. They can check for fingerprints, and so on. But if someone was here, they may have been looking for these."

"A partner in crime, maybe..."

"Aye, perhaps."

The DI walked to the window to look out over the street outside. He saw someone sitting in a black Lexus parked across the road. The Lexus pulled away as he and Susan emerged from the block of flats. McKenzie made a mental note.

When they got back to the station, Graham stood to greet them. "They've found the murder weapon, sir," he said. "It's with forensics... A rock with Caitlin's blood and hair on it. The killer had rolled it down the hill, off the track. They found it in shrubbery."

"Good. Let's hope they find the killer's prints on it, though I suspect they won't. Whoever did this, planned it.

They'll have worn gloves. But they may find fibres if they didn't rub off as it rolled down the hill."

Grant filled Graham in with their passport find at Caitlin's flat.

"Wow, she was a dark horse."

"It seems that way. The plan is to find out more from those who were closest to her. Maybe they can shed light on what she was up to. Can you do me a favour, Graham?"

"Aye."

"Contact the officers supporting her family. I'd like to speak to her loved ones as soon as they are up to it."

"Will do."

4

CAITLIN'S CIRCLE

"Thanks for coming in, Alan." McKenzie greeted Caitlin Murray's ex-boyfriend as a uniformed constable showed him into the interview room.

Alan Bell and Ms Murray had split eight months prior to her murder, and the tall, dark-haired male stared at the DI wide-eyed. "I can't believe I'm here... I mean, I can't believe she's gone. I spoke to her only last week."

Grant took in the man, who evidently kept himself in shape. A professional had given his beard a modern angular cut, such that it tapered to a sharp point when viewed from the side. Like a blade. It was in keeping with the sharp suit he wore, in brown tweed. "It must have been a shock?"

Bell's gaze flicked around the interview room. "It was, and I didn't believe it at first. I hoped it was a case of mistaken identity. I'm still shook, if I'm honest."

"Understandable." McKenzie pulled back a chair for him. "Please, have a seat. We've got a few things to go through with you. We'd like to know who Caitlin was."

"Did she suffer?"

The DI studied Bell's face. "I think she did, though it wouldn't have been for long."

"How was she killed? I mean, with what? Have you found the murder weapon?"

Grant continued staring at Caitlin's ex, his brow furrowed.

The other man cleared his throat.

"I'm afraid I cannot tell you that. It's an ongoing investigation."

"Sure." Bell shrugged.

"Why do you assume the killer used a weapon?"

Alan swallowed. "Well, what with knife crime so prevalent... I just assumed..."

"What do you do, Mr Bell?"

"For a living?"

"Aye."

"My company sources fine wines, and sells it to individuals, restaurants, and other retail chains. We do everything from wines for the connoisseur to table wines for supermarkets. I have warehouses in Edinburgh, London, Manchester, and Cardiff."

"You do all right, then?"

"We do pretty well, yeah. Especially after the pandemic. Our business was already growing, with more people entertaining at home, but COVID sped up that change. We've had our ups and downs, but we're doing great at the moment. Can't complain. We're planning another expansion with a couple of new warehouses in England, and maybe one on the continent. Paris, actually."

"How long were you with Caitlin, and how did you two meet?"

"Er, about five years — give or take."

"So, you knew her pretty well then, eh?"

"Fairly well, yes..."

"You don't sound too sure about that?"

Bell shifted his gaze away towards the door. "Well, she could be..."

"Could be what?"

"Secretive."

"Secretive?"

"Aye, I often felt she was keeping things from me."

"What sort of things?"

Alan shrugged.

"Why do you feel she was keeping things from you, if you cannot name what she was hiding? What made you feel that way?"

"She would go out and not say where she was going or where she had been. She didn't talk about it at all. You know, not even chit-chat. And there'd be trips..."

"Go on..."

"Don't get me wrong, she had to travel to source coffee beans, and I met her on one of those trips, so I canna complain. We were sitting next to each other on the same flight to South America. We swapped numbers." He looked down at the table. "Some of those trips had her really excited and she couldn't wait to talk to me about them; enthusing about the plantations she had been to, the people she met, and the various notes in the aromas of their roasted beans. But there were other trips, which she barely mentioned at all. Only to say the flight was rough, or that she was tired and jet-lagged. And sometimes, I sensed she was downright lying to me."

"Why so?"

"She could be evasive."

"Is that why you split up?"

"I couldn't take it." Bell spat the words, teeth clenched.

McKenzie raised both brows. "Woah, that hit a nerve..."

"I was sure she was seeing someone else. She denied it, of course. But I could see it in her. Why else would she behave like that. I caught her lying about where she'd been one time. She told me she'd been to Venezuela, but she hadn't even left the country. I found the hotel receipt."

"Did you discover why she lied about her whereabouts?"

"I phoned the hotel without telling her. I couldn't trust myself to speak to her about it, but I was so angry."

"What did the hotel say?"

"They said unless I was the law, they wouldn't go into specifics about paying guests."

"Did you catch her out more than once?"

Bell shook his head. "I never found more receipts. She either hid or got rid of them after that time. And I never found out who she might have been with. I did things I'm not proud of, like follow her. But it's like she knew I was there. Whenever I followed her, she went shopping or travelled to one of her clients. You know, coffee shops, warehouses and such."

"Maybe that was all she was ever doing?"

"Then why lie to me? There had to be more to it. No, sadly, I believe there was someone else. And I'd had enough. I would not stay with someone who cheated like that. So, last Easter, I told her I was leaving."

"How did she take it?"

"Well, that was the weird thing."

"Go on..."

"She cried. Oh, not wailing or anything. Not begging me to stay. Just tears rolling down her face. It stopped me in my tracks. Then I reminded myself I couldn't believe a word she said, and I continued packing my bags. And you know what?"

"What?"

"She still didn't talk to me about it. Could not open up. Didn't tell me about the affair. Didn't beg me to stay."

"Did you kill her?"

"What?" Bell scowled at McKenzie. "What do you take me for? I loved the girl. Why would I kill her? Oh, I was angry, sure. I slammed the door on the way out. But I cried myself to sleep a few times, I can tell you. I just didn't understand why it had come to that. I still don't. And I still don't know why she wouldn't talk to me. I felt foolish, like I'd been a doormat."

"Was she cruel?" Grant frowned.

He shook his head, staring at his hands, fingers interlaced. "A part of her was closed off to me — a part I couldn't reach — a segment that probably belonged to someone else. A guy she likely lied to about the times she spent with me."

"Did you feel like hurting her?"

"Maybe, sometimes. Oh, I don't mean killing her... But I sometimes wished I could make her feel the way I felt inside when I discovered she had lied to me about that trip."

"Did you discuss it with her?"

"I questioned her about it. I told her I found the receipt."

"And how did she respond?"

"She was upset I went through her things."

"Did you ask her whether she had been with someone else during that time?"

"I did."

"And had she?"

"She said not, got mad about me checking her purse, and didn't speak to me for two days. She seemed concerned about something. Worried. I think she must have valued the other bloke more than me."

"Why do you say that?"

"Well, I threatened to find him. Threatened to give him a piece of my mind."

"What did she say?"

"Nothing. She just walked out of the flat. She was gone for hours. I felt so angry. When she came back, I couldn't talk to her either. But it was another two or three weeks before I finally decided to leave."

"And how do you feel now?"

"Sad. Confused. I keep wondering why any of it happened. And I wonder who she was. I mean, who she really was." He sighed, his shoulders hunched over.

"Did you ever find out whether there was someone else?"

He shook his head. "No."

"Did you ever follow her again?"

"No. A few times, I picked up my phone and brought up her number. Thought about calling her, or texting. But I didn't call, and I deleted the texts. I just couldn't bring myself to do it. Each time I went soft, I'd remember the lies and the anger would resurface. I'd toss my phone away."

"Did she ever call you?"

"No."

"Where were you at seven am on Tuesday morning?"

"I was in bed."

"Can anyone verify that?"

"My cat."

"Anyone else?"

"No... But I was at my Edinburgh offices by eight-thirty that morning. You can ask my employees, and my secretary. I believe I dealt with emails first thing, too. They will have the times logged. It was a normal week-day morning when I'm not out meeting clients. It was paperwork and decision making. I think they would have noticed if I was in a state because I'd just murdered someone."

The last seemed a little heartless to the DI. "She wasn't just anyone. She was the person you spent five years with."

"Well, even more reason for me to be in a state if I had done something like that."

"You would have had enough time to go home, change, and get to work by eight-thirty..."

"What? If I murdered her? Am I seriously a suspect? We've been apart for months. What motive could I possibly have?"

"Well, you said yourself, you were jealous, and suspicious of her behaviour. Maybe you decided if you couldn't have her, neither could anyone else?"

"I don't think like that. And I didn't kill her. And you have nothing to suggest I did anything wrong, so you can't keep me here."

McKenzie leaned back in his chair. "You're right, I can't. Understand, Mr Bell, I have to ask these questions. It's my job. And if you loved Caitlin, I would hope you understand the need for a thorough investigation to find whoever killed her."

Bell sighed. "Of course... I know that. Am I okay to leave?"

"Yes, but I would ask you to let us know if you intend being out of the area for any significant time. We may need to speak with you again."

∼

Cockburn Street, in Edinburgh's Old Town, gently snaked downhill from High Street to Waverley Station. McKenzie arrived at Ewan MacDonald's coffee shop on foot, deftly negotiating the afternoon throng of wide-eyed tourists and Christmas shoppers.

The Georgian facade, which included large sash windows, gave way to a modern but cosy interior comprising natural materials, such as brick walls, and wooden shelving and countertops, along with the latest lighting and equipment. The aroma of freshly baked pastries and rich coffee teased his nostrils as he gave a nod to the young woman working the espresso machine.

"What can I get you?" she asked, wiping stray strands of straw-blonde hair from her face; one hand on the small of her back.

"I'm looking for Ewan MacDonald? It's Grant McKenzie. He's expecting me."

"Ah, Ewan... He's out back. I'll let him know you're here." She pointed to an empty table in the corner. "Have a seat, if you like."

"I will, thank you." The DI was glad to get off his feet. He eyed the homemade cakes and pastries inside the glass counter, and on the trays atop it. He could almost taste their rich crumbliness.

The girl returned. "Ewan will be through in a minute. Can I get you anything?"

"A plain white coffee, please." He stood to dig the wallet out of his trouser pocket.

The girl held up her hand. "Ewan said, it's on the house." Her eyes flicked to a couple with two young children filing in through the door. "I'll bring it over soon as I can," she said.

"Ach, no rush." McKenzie nodded. "I appreciate it. Thank you."

On the wall next to him, the DI spotted packets of ground coffee and wondered whether Caitlin Murray had sourced and supplied the beans. Her work diary named Ewan and his coffee shop, and she had scheduled a visit to him on the day of her murder.

"Ewan MacDonald." A tall, medium-built male with sandy hair, wearing a pin-striped black apron, held out a large hand.

Grant shook it. "DI Grant McKenzie."

"It's hit us hard, you know... Caitlin..." MacDonald sat opposite the detective.

"I understand her company was one of your main suppliers?"

"Och, she was much more than that, Inspector. We'd been staunch friends for years. She was among the first people I contacted when establishing this place. Caitlin pushed me to expand. Otherwise, I probably would have been too cautious to do it. She was three years younger than me, but she was definitely wiser. I've two more shops in Edinburgh now. I owe that to her."

"When you say friends, were you platonic? Or more than that?" he asked Ewan, before smiling at the young woman who placed his coffee on the table, topped with a fancy froth. "Thank you," he said.

"We were just friends. Nothing more than that. There's a group of us who meet regularly for dinner. We're all in business one way or another and we help push each other forward. We've been close for years. Caitlin, Isla, and Douglas go way back. Myself, and Finlay got to know them later."

The DI took out his notebook. "Sorry, who were the others again?"

"In our group?"

"Yes."

"Well, there was Caitlin and myself."

"How long had you known her?"

"Oh, it must be at least six or seven years? Yes, it would be about that. I was setting up this place, and wanted beans from a local, reputable business. Caitlin had established her coffee company eighteen months to two years prior. But she already had a reputation for excellence. She had a real nose for coffee."

"And the rest of your friends?"

"Isla Campbell had been friends with Caitlin since high school. Isla is a designer for a fashion company called Astrela Maison, specialising in celestial-inspired collections in luxurious fabrics." Ewan grinned. "Or so I am told. They have their headquarters in Paris, and hold shows in most European capitals. Their high-concept evening wear is, I believe, what they're mostly known for. Isla is one of their senior designers, and a bit of a perfectionist. Caitlin's death hit her particularly hard."

"I see... And the others?"

"The other two are Douglas MacNeil and Finlay Scott. Douglas is a GP, here in Edinburgh. He lived next door to Caitlin when they were little. They grew up together and dated each other in high school. They ended their relationship because they were both ambitious and thought a long-distance relationship would be unlikely to work. While Caitlin studied business in Edinburgh, MacNeil studied medicine in London."

"And Finlay Scott?"

"Finlay teaches English to high school kids and plays squash with Douglas. I think he's in love with Isla, but she sees him only as a friend. And we are all good friends, and Caitlin's murder has been hard to fathom. We have thought about little else, you ken? She was a lovely lass. I am devastated by her loss. The last few days have been hard. I can't concentrate on anything."

"And Caitlin was still sourcing coffee for you?"

"Aye, she was. She would regularly introduce me to new varieties and new ways of roasting. She travelled all over Central and South America, Africa, and Asia, exploring growing and roasting methods. That girl was superb with the local people and many of them took her to their hearts. And she was always bringing me back samples to try, and my customers have been so used to me advertising a new 'coffee of the month'. Some come in just for that. This month we've been showcasing a sweet and nutty variety from Thailand. I thought it would be a good one for Christmas. But it won't be the same now... Not without Caitlin. It's hard to enthuse about anything. When I get choked up, I go out back."

"That's understandable."

"We all had dinner only last week."

"And how did Caitlin appear at dinner?"

"She was her usual self. Nothing out of the ordinary. We all chatted like we always do."

"Have you any idea who may have wanted to hurt her?" McKenzie studied Ewan's face.

"Do you think someone targeted her?"

"We don't know."

He opened his mouth. "I-" He closed it again.

"Yes?"

Ewan cleared his throat. "I have no idea."

"You were about to say something."

"No... No." He shrugged. "I can't help you, Inspector."

"Do you ever wear aftershave?"

"What?"

"Aftershave?"

"No, why?"

"Do you know anyone else who wears aftershave?"

"Douglas and Finlay use it, occasionally. Sometimes to dinner. It's never been my thing, I'm afraid."

"Would you write the contact details of her other friends in here for me?" The DI turned to a clean page in his notebook and handed it to the other man.

"Sure." Ewan pulled a pen from his shirt pocket and scribbled on the pad. "There you go. That's everybody."

"Very good." McKenzie checked his watch. "I'd better be off. Thank you for the coffee." He stood. "And I am very sorry for your loss."

"Do you think you'll find Caitlin's killer, Inspector?"

"We'll do everything in our power to bring them to justice, aye. There are no guarantees in life, but we'll do everything we can to catch the perpetrator. Have a good evening, Ewan."

"Thanks. You, too."

∼

As McKenzie walked away from the coffee shop, back towards High Street, he felt the hackles rise on his back as though he was being followed, and turned to look at the other people on the street going about their daily business. No-one was looking, and there was nobody close. He gave himself a mental shake and made his way back to the car. He had just about enough time to get back to the office and type up his notes before heading home.

5

AN UNEXPECTED DEATH

Caitlin's parents, John and Stephanie Murray, lived in a two-bed apartment in Clifton Mews, off the Baileyfield Road in Portobello, and near Figgate Park, four miles east of Edinburgh city centre. In their mid-sixties, they had downsized from a larger family home two years prior.

McKenzie parked in the residents' car park without a permit, John having assured him over the phone it would be fine, and waited at the automatic door to be let in. He understood why the Murrays had chosen the area. It sported beautiful sea walks and an award-winning beach, plentiful restaurants, and an excellent bus network to and from the city centre.

John Murray looked as though he hadn't slept since losing Caitlin. Deep shadows underscored his red-rimmed eyes as he led the DI into a spacious lounge with windows overlooking the garden.

His wife sat in an armchair, looking lost as she stared through the window, deep in thought.

"Please, take a seat." John pointed to a duck-egg-blue fabric sofa as he chose the remaining armchair.

"Thank you for seeing me." McKenzie regarded them both. "I know this is a difficult time for you. I want you to know how very sorry we are for your loss, and my team and I will work tirelessly to find your daughter's killer."

A tear wended its way down Stephanie's cheek as she continued staring out over the sparse winter garden.

"We appreciate that, Inspector." John Murray sighed, shaking his head. "I don't get it. Who would want to hurt our beautiful daughter. She wouldna have harmed a fly."

"That's a question I wanted to ask you..." McKenzie pulled out his notebook. "Were you aware of anyone with a grudge against Caitlin? We're struggling to find a motive. We determined it was neither a robbery nor a sexual assault. How did she get on with her ex-partner? And did she have anyone else on the scene romantically?"

John shook his head. "I don't think she was seeing anyone else yet. And Alan, well... What a waste of space he turned out to be. But hurting her? I canna say I could see him doing that... though he was always suspicious of her, right enough. He left her because he thought she was cheating. She was fair upset, but she wouldn't have taken him back."

"Why not?"

"She believed in honouring commitments, and in unconditional love."

"I understand Caitlin travelled a lot with her business?"

"For the coffee? Aye, she was never happier than when she was meeting new folks and finding the best coffees she could. And you know, we used to worry like crazy when she was off in those far-flung places, praying she would come home in one piece. And there she was, only going for a morning run in her home city, and... and..."

"And someone murdered her."

"Aye, some bastard murdered her."

"John, language," Stephanie admonished.

"Well, it's true."

"It's okay." The DI cocked his head. "Strong language is perfectly justified in the circumstances. I'd be swearing, too." He turned to John. "Were you aware of Caitlin ever travelling under a false identity?"

Mr Murray frowned. "False identity? I don't understand. Why would she do that?"

"I don't know, yet."

"Are you saying she did?"

"We found several fake passports at her home."

"False passports?" John pulled a face.

Stephanie stared at McKenzie. "She-"

John shot his wife a look.

Mrs Murray turned back to the window.

"You were going to say something?" The DI looked from Stephanie to her husband and back.

"I had a thought, but it's nothing."

"Really?" he pressed.

"We don't know why she would have had the fake passports," John interjected. "Maybe she wanted to keep a low profile."

"Why would she want to do that?"

"Maybe to avoid people like the person who killed her?" John scowled. "I'd like to get my hands on whoever it was."

"I'd appreciate it if you didn't mention the passports to anyone, for now. I agree, she may have had a perfectly legitimate reason for having them. But are you telling me you didn't know she travelled with them?"

"We've never heard of her doing that, have we, Steph?"

His wife shook her head. "It makes no sense to me."

"Did your daughter ever mention being afraid of anyone? Or tell you anyone was pestering her?"

"No, she didn't."

"When did you last see her?"

"It was Thursday evening. Last Thursday."

"And how did she seem?"

"She seemed fine. Happy enough, and it sounded like her work was keeping her busy. If she had any inkling she was in danger, she didn't show it."

"I see. And how often did she travel abroad?"

"On average, I would say once a month. Sometimes it was more; sometimes less."

"And she never mentioned going incognito?"

"No." John flicked a look at his wife.

McKenzie was sure they were hiding something from him. "Are you sure now? I want you to think very carefully about your answers. They could mean the difference between us catching your daughter's killer or never finding them."

Mr Murray cleared his throat. "We can't tell you any more, Inspector. As much as we might have wanted to, we didn't know everything about our daughter. Everyone has things they keep private. Why would it be different for Caitlin?"

The DI looked over at Stephanie, knowing there was more she wanted to say. He pressed his lips together. "Very well. Here is my card. I want you to call me if you remember anything else. If Caitlin did anything... anything she later regretted, it would still be important for me to know about it as it might be a factor in her murder. If she knew dodgy people, for instance, or if she was running errands for them under assumed identities, I would still be more interested in solving her murder and catching those responsible than sullying her name."

"I'll show you out, Inspector." John rose to his feet. "We'll have a think about it and let you know if we remember anything we ought to tell you."

"Thank you." McKenzie stood, following Murray as he led him back to the front door.

"Watch how you go, Inspector." John called after the DI's back.

Grant turned around to reply, but he had closed the door.

Watching his breath cloud in the icy air, the DI heard an engine fire up on the street outside. The vehicle sat there ticking over for a couple of minutes before driving away. A black Lexus, similar to the one he had seen outside of Caitlin's flat. Grant heard it leave as he opened the door of his own car. Was this significant? Or a coincidence? And what of Caitlin's parents? He felt they were keeping something from him. Exactly what had Caitlin Murray got herself mixed up in?

∼

"THE WANDERER RETURNS." Graham grinned at McKenzie as the latter walked in. "Is it snowing out there?"

The DI brushed his shoulders, cold and wet from melted flakes, before placing his coat on a hook near the door. "Aye, it started about ten minutes ago. It's coming down thick now."

"I'll get you a brew, and we can bring you up to speed with what we've been up to."

As the DI sipped his tea, grateful for its warmth, Graham brought over a printout of Caitlin's mobile phone records.

"Right, what are we looking at?" McKenzie asked, eyeing the paragraphs ringed with red marker.

"Caitlin was making regular calls to this number." Graham tapped the paper.

Grant could see that most of the highlighted calls were to the same phone.

"And occasionally, she received a call back from that number."

"Good work. Whose phone is it?" McKenzie pored over the data.

"We don't know. The phone company won't tell us."

"What?"

"They are refusing to give us that information. They said they can't."

"What if we get a court order?"

"Well, that's just it. They are telling us they cannot disclose for reasons of national security."

"National security?"

"Aye."

"So, whatever Caitlin got herself mixed up in, it was pretty serious stuff?"

"Looks like it."

"Was she smuggling? Some countries she visited have serious issues with gangs involved in moving people and drugs."

"True enough, but why would a phone company withhold the identity of a smuggling gang member?"

"Maybe they've been told to? If there's a high-level operation in progress, undercover stuff, that would be highly sensitive information."

"Of course." Dalgleish nodded.

"So maybe a serious crime squad is involved, or the intelligence services?" McKenzie pushed his hands into his pockets, thinking.

"They would want things under wraps."

"And they may be surveilling whoever Caitlin was in contact with." McKenzie's eyes widened. "Or Caitlin was working for the intelligence services."

"Right." Graham nodded. "That is a possibility. I mean, there aren't many smugglers who change their identity like that."

"I wonder if Caitlin was a spook?"

"Or if she was helping them... That could be why the phone company is stonewalling us."

"And one of these operations got her killed..."

"A travelling business woman buying coffee beans would be the perfect cover. Who'd suspect her of gathering intelligence? And she had excellent connections in South America and other parts..."

"Bloody hell."

"Aye, exactly." Dalgleish sat back, rubbing the back of his head. "Puts a unique spin on it all, doesn't it?"

"Aye it does," McKenzie agreed. "Get on to our contacts in SOCT," he said, referring to the Serious Organised Crime Taskforce in Scotland. "Find out if they know of ongoing operations involving Caitlin Murray."

"Aye, I'll start digging." Dalgleish folded the phone printout, carrying it back to his desk.

∼

GRAHAM FLICKED through his contact list, looking for an old friend in SOCT. The stonewalling from the phone company had been infuriating, but the mention of "national security" had them thinking there had to be a lot more to Caitlin's story. Something wasn't right.

DI Iain Kerr had crossed paths with their team on a joint operation a few years before, and his no-nonsense attitude had left an impression. If anyone could give them a lead, it was Kerr.

Dialling his number, Dalgleish leaned back in his chair, clearing his throat as the call connected. "Sir, it's Graham Dalgleish, from Edinburgh MIT. How's it going?"

"Dalgleish? Bloody hell, it's been a while. What brings you to my door? Not another Edinburgh-Stirling derby bust-up, I hope."

The DC laughed. "Not quite... We're working a murder, one Caitlin Murray. Someone bludgeoned her to death in Corstorphine Woods. I need some info, and I reckon you may be the man to help."

Kerr hesitated. "I'll do what I can, but murders aren't usually my playground. What's the connection to SOCT?"

"Call records, Iain. The victim was in contact with a number we can't trace. And the phone company's clammed up, citing national security. It's got to be big if they're blanking us like this."

"National security, you say? Christ, you sure you want to be poking at this? Sounds like something that could bite you back."

"I don't have a choice. We've got a dead woman, multiple passports in different names which she used to go back and forth to South America and places, and a feeling this wasn't a run-of-the-mill killing. If there's something going on, I need to know. Was she being watched by one of your lot?"

Kerr sighed. "Look, Graham, I'll tell you what I can, but I've got my limits, you know that. We've heard whispers of an embedded asset in certain circles; someone gathering intelligence. But if you're asking me if it involved your victim, I can't confirm that. It's above my pay grade, and yours too."

The DC leaned forward, frustration knitting his brows. "Look, I need more, sir. You're telling me you've heard whispers of something going on, but you can't help me connect the dots? I thought you guys would be easier than the bloody phone company."

"Hey, calm down. I get that you're frustrated. But they don't send memos to SOCT for this sort of thing. If she was under surveillance by, say, MI5 or MI6, they wouldn't tell us any more than they needed to. Maybe she was being watched. Maybe she wasn't. My advice? Keep digging, but tread carefully."

"Are you saying this could blow back on me if I press too hard?"

"Not just you, but your entire investigation. It sounds like you have a dangerous thread in your hands. Pull it, and you might unravel more than you bargained for."

Dalgleish exhaled, running a hand through his hair. "Cheers for the warning, Iain. I'll let you know what we find when we shake the tree."

"Aye, just don't get crushed by what falls out. Take care, Graham. Give my best to McKenzie."

∽

"Everything okay?" Grant walked over to Dalgleish's desk.

"Oh aye, everything's dandy, except I cannae get anything out of anyone. Why does everyone get crabbit over this case? And what's with all the cloak-and-dagger stuff?" He outlined his conversation with Iain Kerr to the DI.

"We're supposed to be on the same team, but it sometimes doesn't feel like it."

"I'm not surprised you hit a wall there, Graham. Information at that level, especially when it comes to the intelligence services, is compartmentalised. They rarely know what each other is working on, let alone telling us what's going on. I'll try official channels, speak to Sinclair, and ask that we put in a formal request for information from MI5 or MI6. I can't promise anything, but at least they'll know who is making the request and why. Something tells me Caitlin Murray got herself caught up in something she couldn't get out of. If she was involved with a smuggling racket and gangs working out of South America, she would know the danger she was in. Perhaps that is why she lived so lightly. Maybe she was prepared to run at a moment's notice. Travelling regularly to that part of the world was bound to raise eyebrows, but SOCT wouldn't necessarily know everything the intelligence services know about the gangs."

"Aye, fair enough."

"I think Caitlin's parents know more than they are letting on. When they have had time to come to terms with their daughter's death, I'll be speaking to them again. I really felt there was more they wanted to say. I think Caitlin got herself mixed up in something she couldn't get out of, and lost her life as a result. A gang may have coerced her into smuggling under assumed identities, for fear of losing her business if she didn't. Either way, we have to get to the bottom of what was going on."

∽

HELEN MCALLISTER WHISTLED through her teeth as she put the phone down. "Grant, we have another death."

"What?"

"Someone found a body among the trees near Duddingston Kirk," she answered, referring to a church in King's Park, on the east side of Edinburgh.

"Did they say it was a murder?"

"They said a suspicious death, yes."

"We'd better get over there. Who's free?"

"I'll come," Dalgleish answered. "I need to stretch my back, anyway. It's been giving me problems all morning."

"That'll be the stiff wind. Are you sure you'll be all right out there?"

The DC grimaced. "Aye, it's these online searches that are doing my back. I prefer being out there, in the thick of it."

"Fine." McKenzie grinned. "Come on then, old man."

6

WORRIED FRIENDS

Snow was still falling, but it had thinned to the occasional flake. The wind had whipped it into uneven piles as they approached the crime scene through the trees near the kirk. Beyond the twelfth century building lay one of the last remaining natural lochs in Edinburgh, Duddingston Loch.

The body lay amid the trees leading down to the water from the kirk, and SOCO were already erecting a tent over the scene, which they had cordoned off. The area was otherwise quiet, there being no onlookers to speak of.

McKenzie and Dalgleish received plastic suits and overshoes from the officers securing the area, and put them on.

The DI recognised immediately the similarities between the victim's bludgeoning and Caitlin's. But this victim wasn't a runner. He was dressed in jeans, an outdoor jacket, and leather shoes. "Do we know who he is?" he asked the forensic officer, who was busy writing notes.

The officer shook his head. "Not yet."

The victim lay on his left side, almost in the recovery position, but his right arm was outstretched along the ground as though reaching for something. Congealed blood covered the right side of his head, obscuring his features.

McKenzie, in forensic suit and overshoes, walked around to the front of the victim; kneeling to peer into the man's face. "Bloody hell," he rocked back on his heels. "That's Ewan MacDonald. I was speaking to him only yesterday. How in the world did he end up here, like this?"

"Is it Caitlin's friend?" Dalgleish frowned.

"Aye, it is. And if I was a betting man, I'd say he was killed by the same attacker. He looks to have been bashed on the head in the same way Caitlin was. Well, this has thrown me a bit. I wasn't expecting this." McKenzie got to his feet, stepping back to allow forensic officers to continue with their work.

"Did he seem scared when you spoke to him yesterday?"

"No, he didn't. He gave me the names of his close-knit friends, names that included Caitlin..." The DI closed his eyes for a moment. "I felt at one point he was about to tell me something about her murder, but changed his mind. I was going to tell you before we got the call about his murder. This man was very close to Caitlin. She persuaded him to expand his business. He was really excited about opening two new cafes in Edinburgh. It seems he and Caitlin encouraged and supported each other's businesses."

"Maybe he knew what she had gotten herself mixed up in?"

"Aye, maybe. You know, Graham, I had the distinct feeling someone was following me yesterday. I saw a black Lexus. I don't know, maybe I am seeing those cars more now I am conscious of them, but I have seen a black Lexus several times outside of places connected with this case."

"Did you get the registration?"

"No."

"If you see it again, get the plate number. I'll run a check."

"How long has this man been dead, would you say?" McKenzie asked the nearest SOCO.

"Only a couple of hours, given the external temperature. But you'll get a better estimate from the pathologist."

"Is Fiona on her way?" he asked, referring to the pathologist.

"She should be. No word on when she'll get here, though. I recorded the temperatures when I arrived."

"Good." The DI nodded. "If she is not here by the time we leave, tell her I'll speak to her later today."

"I'll let her know." The forensic officer got back to work.

∽

Isla Campbell was the last to arrive at The Dome, an upmarket bar in George Street, whose Georgian facade, complete with four Corinthian-style pillars at the door, gave way to a sumptuous interior that would not look amiss in a lavish stately home. A central round bar, topped with a massive Christmas tree lit by thousands of LED lights, greeted those who entered. The domed ceiling, patterned and inlaid with glass panels, added to the opulence of the place.

Tall and wiry; auburn bob streaked with highlights, Isla glided between the tables in a tight red dress and black overcoat, her walk exaggerated like that of a catwalk model. Bright nail polish, red lipstick, and visible eye make-up finished her ensemble. She had the air of someone from a bygone era, but one you wouldn't mess with. Isla Campbell knew who she was and where she was going, and she would decide if that journey included you.

Finlay Scott, on the other hand, did not feel at all confident tonight. He swallowed frequently, flicking his eyes around the restaurant as though expecting trouble at any moment. His hand trembled as he lifted a wineglass to his lips, his lean frame hunched over. He straightened up, however, when he saw Isla approach, smoothing his sandy hair and clearing his throat.

"Finlay." Isla nodded the greeting before turning her gaze to his companion. "Douglas."

"Hello, Isla." Douglas MacNeil's smile didn't reach his eyes. The muscles in his face were stiff as he darted a glance towards the bar. "We thought we would wait for you before ordering."

"Thanks." She placed her jacket over the back of a chair before pulling it out and sitting. "I have to say, after what's happened... I'm not that hungry."

"Me neither," Finlay agreed. "I don't think I could eat a thing."

"Well, I wasn't hungry, but I've had the busy day from hell, and I need to eat before I keel over." Douglas pulled a face, his square jaw hidden as he read the menu. "But I'm having trouble deciding."

"Douglas," Isla hissed. "Ewan is dead. Caitlin is dead."

"I know." He turned his handsome face back to hers, his tone the same one he used on his patients. "But we cannot change that. And if I don't eat, I may join them." He relented upon seeing her open mouth. "Look, I am as shocked as you. And I agree we all need to talk, but I can eat and think at the same time. Otherwise, why meet here? We might just as well have gone to a pub."

Isla grimaced. "That would not have been appropriate."

"Then sit. We'll order food, those of us that want some..." He glanced at Finlay. "And then we can talk."

After giving their orders, Isla glared at Douglas. "Well? What do we do now?" She wondered if he ever dropped his general practitioner facade. It had never irked her before, but it did this evening. She turned her gaze to Finlay. He appeared completely out of his depth, like he could bolt out the door if someone so much as breathed on him. She turned back to Douglas. "Aren't you scared?"

He sipped his wine. "Yes, a little, of course. But we cannot let whoever is doing this know that. We have to go to the police. We should have done so at the beginning."

"Yes, but we didn't know the threats were serious. How could we? I've been trolled before. I thought this was the same thing. Clearly, it wasn't."

"And I thought you were merely afraid of whatever secrets this killer troll had on you."

"Douglas..." It was Finlay's turn to stare at his friend, slack-jawed. "We can't turn on each other. It's probably what they want, whoever is doing this. And they likely don't have any secrets of ours to tell. It's probably a psychopath messing with us."

Douglas turned to Finlay. "Except Caitlin was afraid of something being revealed, wasn't she? Wasn't it she who persuaded us all to hold back from going to police in the first place? She seemed worried about the mischief this person could do." He looked at Isla. "She was your best friend. You should have convinced her to go to the authorities."

Isla choked back a sob. "God, I wish I had. I really wish..." She dropped her gaze to the table. "And I agree. I think it's time we took those letters to police. I didn't sleep last night. Too busy thinking about Caitlin and Ewan lying cold on the ground. I can't bear the thought of..." She struggled to finish her sentence. "They had their heads caved in. What kind of sick person does that?"

"The kind that sends these..." Douglas glanced around the restaurant, checking they hadn't drawn attention to themselves, before pulling out a letter from his pocket. "Perhaps the police can still get DNA from the letters."

"But we've all handled them." Finlay pulled a face. "That's going to complicate things a bit."

"We will have to give our DNA, of course. But they can take it

into account and get the killer's profile from whatever is left." MacNeil shrugged.

"What if the killer wore gloves and they can't catch him? What then?"

"Another of us gets murdered." MacNeil put the letter back in his pocket. "We cannot let that happen. We'll go together. Tomorrow. I'll call in sick. I suggest you two do the same. We'll meet at the station. Are you in agreement?"

Isla nodded.

"Yes, all right." Finlay put his head in his hands. "Anything to stop this madness."

7

DIFFICULT CONVERSATIONS

Grant eyed the DCI's cluttered desk as Rob Sinclair regarded him silently. The DI loosened his tie, not sure what to expect.

"So, you want to go digging around with the intelligence services? Are you sure that's a good idea? I mean, they're not likely to be forthcoming."

"I don't see we have much choice, Rob. There was more to Caitlin than her coffee company. Like I said, we found multiple passports in various identities. And Helen discovered unexplained payments to Murray's bank accounts that are proving difficult to trace back to source. There were frequent trips abroad, many to South America, that her need to source new products could satisfactorily explain, but that need wouldn't explain the passports."

"Do you know if she actually used the other passports?"

McKenzie nodded. "They are each stamped with at least two countries she visited."

Sinclair rubbed the stubble on his chin. "I admit, that is odd; suspicious even, but none of that proves her murder had anything to do with gang related crime, or MI5 or MI6."

"True, but I believe it's a good place to start. Look, if the intelligence services were following her, or someone in the shadows thought they were, they might have wanted her silenced or out of the picture. We know those gangs don't mess about. She may have drawn attention to herself, whether or not she knew it, and the people she was working for could have noticed. Put it this way, someone taking frequent trips with multiple passports is going to attract attention. I think talking to someone in MI5 could, at the very least, give us a clearer picture of her movements and contacts. Right now, I'm working blind. I agree, her death may be unrelated to whatever she was up to. Perhaps she did simply meet the wrong person at the wrong time up there in Corstophine Woods. And, maybe, one of her best friends did as well, down at Duddingston Loch. But, honestly? I don't think that's likely, and I cannot see the harm in digging deeper."

Sinclair steepled his hands under his chin. "I hear you. But you realise you're wading into murky waters. If this blows back on us, the brass upstairs won't be happy. If there is an ongoing operation, these things can be delicate. They won't want extra attention brought to it. Nothing must reach local news outlets. You cannot jeopardise whatever it is they have going on."

"I understand, sir. And I know the risks. I trust my team to tread carefully through this. But time is of the essence. We must pursue this line of enquiry, because the killer could strike again; if there's even a chance her death was connected to her activities abroad, we owe it to her and the public. We've already lost one of her friends to the same killer. The MO was the identical. They were both daytime murders, where the perp used a heavy object to bash the victim's skull in. All I know is Caitlin was making calls to, and receiving calls from, a number which her telephone company refuses to give details for. That tells me there is likely an intelligence op around whatever she was up to. Graham received a cryptic nod in that direction, too, when he contacted SOCT. I say we instigate a formal enquiry with the intelligence services and see what they say."

Sinclair drummed his fingers on the desk. "Okay, fine. But go through the proper channels. And keep me in the loop. I don't want any surprises."

"Understood, sir. Thank you. I'll let you know what they say."

∼

BACK BEHIND HIS DESK, McKenzie dialled the contact number for MI5 in London, waiting for someone to pick up. After several rings, and a couple of rounds of multiple-choice questions because he didn't know the extension he required, a woman's clipped voice answered.

"Good afternoon, this is switchboard. Do you know the extension you require?"

"Er, no, I'm afraid I don't." McKenzie kept his frustration in check. "I'm DI Grant McKenzie, Police Scotland. I need to speak with someone regarding a murder investigation we are conducting in connection with one Caitlin Murray."

"One moment, Detective Inspector. Please hold."

The line clicked to music, mechanical and distant. A piece designed to calm and possibly uplift. It failed on all counts. After an excruciating wait, a male baritone voice answered in received pronunciation.

"Detective Inspector McKenzie? I'm Agent Riley from the Security Service. I understand you're enquiring about someone called Caitlin Murray?"

"That is correct, sir. She was murdered last week here in Edinburgh. And during our investigation, we identified the following lines of enquiry: multiple passports, overseas travel to hotspots, and unexplained financial activity. When we made enquiries over regular calls she made and received, we hit a roadblock with her phone service provider over one number in particular. That has given us to believe she may have been the subject of surveillance, or an intelligence operation of some kind."

"Hence your call to us..."

"Hence my call to you, sir, yes."

Riley hesitated. "I'm afraid I cannot confirm or deny anything regarding an operation involving Ms Murray."

"Look, I understand your need for caution. However, I'm investigating not only Caitlin's murder. We think the same killer murdered one of her close friends. Your withholding of information could impede our investigation and put others in danger if an MI5 operation is involved."

"I understand that, Detective Inspector, and I can only assure you that matters concerning national security are being handled appropriately. I cannot comment further, I'm afraid."

"Can you confirm whether she was being watched?"

A sigh emanated from the other end.

"Look, I just need her movements in the days before her death. If this is unrelated to your work, say so, and I'll move on."

"I'm sorry, DI McKenzie, but I'm unable to assist. I suggest you carry out your murder investigation in the usual way. If you have any other inquiries, please direct them through your DCI."

"You're stonewalling me. People's lives are at stake."

"This conversation is over, Detective Inspector. Good day."

The line died, leaving McKenzie gripping the receiver, knuckles white.

∽

"Are you okay?" Helen McAllister headed over to Grant's desk.

"Och, Helen, I don't know why things have to be so bloody... difficult."

He headed straight back to Sinclair's office and stood, arms crossed, recounting the conversation he had with Riley. "It was like talking to a brick wall. All I got was deflection and bureaucratic nonsense. He wouldna even confirm if she was subject to surveillance. How are we supposed to move forward under those circumstances? And how can I get to the bottom of whatever it was she was up to, if I can't get her phone company to tell me anything about the number she called the day before she died? The mystery number appears throughout her printout. Calls to and from a person who cannot be named, apparently."

"Ach, come on, Grant. You didn't expect them to roll out the red carpet, did you?"

"Of course not, but I expected... something. An acknowledgment, at least."

"So, what is your plan now?"

"We have no choice. We keep digging. If they won't help us, we'll find another way to piece together Caitlin's story. Someone out there knows what she was involved in. We just have to find them before the killer does."

The DCI nodded. "Well, if I can help in any way, let me know."

"Thanks." Grant sighed. "Riley said if we needed to call again, we were to go through you. Maybe you would have more luck, eh?"

"I'd be willing to make that call for you, but get me more. Give me something that confirms she was involved in smuggling or similar, and I will make that phone call. At least, then, we'll have their attention."

"Aye, I'll do what I can, Rob. And thanks."

"No problem."

8

THE FRIENDS

McKenzie was busy recounting his conversations with Sinclair and Riley to the other members of his team, when a call through from the front desk to tell him a woman named Isla Campbell was in reception demanding to see the lead detective involved in the Caitlin Murray and Ewan MacDonald murder investigations.

"Isla Campbell? I recognise that name." He frowned. "She was friends with Ewan and Caitlin. Is she there now?" he asked the civilian receptionist.

"She says she's not leaving until she's spoken with you."

Grant thought perhaps he should have tried the same tactic on Riley. "Okay, tell her we'll be right down."

"Want some help?" Dalgleish got up from his desk.

"Aye, that would be helpful. Let's see what Ms Campbell has to say for herself. It sounds important."

Isla stood next to the front desk, examining her nails; a stern look on her face.

"Ms Campbell?" McKenzie asked as he and Dalgleish approached.

"I thought murder investigations were urgent affairs?" She eyed him with disdain.

"They are. We came as fast as we could, but we cannot simply drop everything we are doing each time someone demands to see us, Ms Campbell. We'd get nowhere if we did."

"Very well." She sighed. "You can call me Isla." She held out a well-manicured hand. "I'm sorry. I don't wish for us to get off on the wrong foot."

"No problem, Isla." The DI shook the offered hand. "If you come with us, we'll go somewhere we can talk properly."

They led her to an interview room and told her to take a seat.

Dalgleish set two files and a notebook down on the table.

"So, what brings you here to see us today?" McKenzie leaned back in his seat, regarding the fashion designer with an inquisitive eye. She appeared self-assured, and as though she wouldn't suffer fools gladly, but there was something else in her eyes. Fear, perhaps.

She leaned forward. "Two of my best friends are dead, and we are already going through a hellish time, but I had to show you this." She took a folded piece of paper from her coat pocket, opening it up on the desk, and smoothing it flat. She turned it towards the detectives. "I, and my friends, received these three weeks before Caitlin's and Ewan's deaths."

It was a typed letter addressed to Isla. "You say your friends received one of these, too?"

"We all did, including Caitlin and Ewan. And they are now dead."

"Hmm..." McKenzie donned nitrile gloves from a box on the edge of the desk. "May I?"

"Of course." She pushed it towards him.

As the DI read, it became clear the writer of the letter was angry, telling the recipients they had gone too far and there would be consequences. The author had stopped short of saying what those consequences would be, or even what they had done, but left the reader in no doubt there would be a price to pay.

"And when did you receive this? There's no date on it." McKenzie turned it over and back as though to double-check.

"About a month ago. It was three weeks before someone killed Caitlin; presumably the person who wrote this."

"They addressed this letter specifically to you. Was it the same with your friend's letters? Were they referred to by name?"

"Yes, we were all addressed by name in the letters, including Caitlin and Ewan."

"How many of you received this?"

"Five."

"Can you give me all the names, Isla?"

"There was myself, obviously, Caitlin, Ewan, Douglas MacNeil, and Finlay Scott."

Dalgleish jotted the names down on his notepad.

"And yo are all very close friends," the DI stated.

"Yes... How did you know?"

"That you were all friends? Ewan MacDonald told me, in the days following Caitlin's death."

"Oh, I see." The corners of her mouth turned down. "I cannot believe that two of our friends are gone." She pointed to the letter. "And there must be a connection."

"What did you think when you got these letters?" he asked. "Ewan never mentioned receiving one."

"Maybe he wasn't sure whether to report it?"

"Even after Caitlin's murder?" McKenzie's brow furrowed. "Were you not afraid the writer of these threats had begun acting on them?"

She grimaced. "We didn't take the threats seriously at first. I mean, we are all successful in our own way. That can sometimes attract the wrong sort of attention. Trolls... You know? I wrongly assumed there was nothing to worry about. Envy makes some people act in nasty ways. I thought the sender was likely deranged, but I suspected the threats were empty." She sighed and continued. "When Caitlin was killed, I thought she was probably in the wrong place at the wrong time. Women sometimes get hurt in parks or on trails. It's not unheard of. But now, with Ewan's murder quickly following, we are bound to take these letters seriously. Looks like whoever wrote them meant business."

"Have you any idea who sent them to you and your pals?"

She shook her head. "We none of us have any idea. We really don't. And we're terrified, obviously."

"We will have to keep this." McKenzie studied the woman's face. "For forensic testing."

"Of course." She nodded.

Graham stood. "I'll fetch an evidence bag."

"Do the others still have their letters, Isla?"

She nodded, clasping her hands together. "We all kept them, even though none of us took them seriously at first.

Caitlin believed we should hang on to them... in case." She lowered her lids. "But I honestly didn't think this psycho would actually kill any of us."

"The sender seems angered by something you've done. Any idea what they are referring to?"

Isla shook her head. "I have no idea. And I have wracked my brains to think of something, believe me. After Caitlin and Ewan were murdered, I've had a few sleepless nights, I can tell you. It's no joke, thinking you could be next. I am wary of every corner now; every shadow. I'm turning into a nervous wreck."

"I understand you are a designer for Astrela Maison." he said, placing the letter into the evidence bag Graham handed to him.

"That's right."

"How long have you worked for them?"

"It's been a few years."

"Have you had any arguments, or problems with anyone else working there, or anyone associated with the business?"

She shook her head. "Not that I can think of, and certainly nothing serious. I doubt anyone working for the fashion house would have sent us something like this."

"You said Caitlin received one of these letters."

"Yes, she did."

"What happened to it?"

Isla's eyes widened. "I don't know. I would have expected it to be somewhere in her flat."

"We didn't find any such letter during our search of her home. Did she throw it away?"

She frowned. "I suppose it's possible, but we all agreed to keep our copies in case anything happened. We agreed it would be wise to save them as evidence."

"And Caitlin agreed?"

"Yes, I think it was Caitlin who suggested it." She frowned. "Or maybe it was Douglas? I was all for throwing them in the bin, so was Finlay. He gets anxious about these things. But Douglas thought the sender might do something ridiculous like key one of our cars or something. That is the level we were viewing this at, like someone was upset and having a rant. We never thought they would actually harm any of us."

"I guess that's understandable."

"How wrong were we?" She hung her head.

"You weren't to know." The DI leaned forward. "I wish you had come to us sooner, but your reaction wouldn't be unusual. So don't beat yourself up about it. You have come to us now, and that is the important thing. These letters could help us solve your friends' murders. We'll send this for forensics, and we would also like to have the copies sent to Douglas MacNeil and Finlay Scott."

"I'll let them know," she said. "But I believe they want to talk to you, too."

"Good, because we should like to speak to them."

"Douglas hasn't had it easy, what with his wife running off with another man not long after they were married, and now two of his best friends being murdered. And Finlay, well, he's afraid of his own shadow now."

McKenzie nodded. "Don't worry, Isla. I shall speak to both of them as soon as possible. In the meantime, if you have any concerns at all, I want you to call me on this number." He passed her a card. "Stay vigilant, and aware of your surroundings. Don't walk anywhere alone after dark and make sure people know where you are. Any concerns, and we can put people outside your house. In the meantime, we will have officers doing extra beats and drive-bys at your home and work address. We can do the same for your friends until we find whoever wrote this."

"Thank you, Inspector." Isla made to get up.

"One more thing." Grant cocked his head. "Did Caitlin ever talk to you about her trips abroad?"

"In what way?"

"Did she ever tell you what she'd been up to while away?" McKenzie studied Isla's face, watching her reactions.

"She told me about people she met and new coffee crops she was excited about. Most of her trips were about coffee. I have to confess to switching off. Though I loved how enthusiastic she was, and I enjoy a coffee, I just didn't have the same level of interest she had. I guess she felt the same about fashion."

"Did she ever talk about risky situations or meeting dangerous people?"

"What? In the coffee trade? No. Do you think the killer is someone in the coffee business?"

He held up a hand. "No, I'm not saying that. We don't know who killed your friends yet. But think about conversations she had with you. Did she have any concerns, or discuss difficulties she had while abroad."

"I can't recall anything off the top of my head," she replied. "But I will think about it and let you know."

"On your way out, an officer will take a cheek swab from you. Is that okay? We'll need it to rule your DNA out from any profiles we develop from the letter."

"Oh yes, of course." She smiled. "I'll make sure I give a sample."

"Perfect, thank you." McKenzie showed the designer to the door. "Call us with any concerns."

"I will, Inspector."

∼

"Do you think the writer of that letter is the killer?" Dalgleish frowned. "Whoever it is, they don't seem the full shilling."

"That's my thought, Graham," the DI agreed. "It's almost like they are trying too hard... The letter is over the top."

"Do you think she wrote it to herself?"

"Not necessarily, but something is off." McKenzie shrugged. "We'll ask the other friends for their copies and get their stories. Let's find out who these people really are. In the meantime, I want someone to re-examine Caitlin's flat before it's cleared. If one of these letters is somewhere in that flat, I want it as soon as possible."

"I'll organise another search." Dalgleish nodded. "Leave it with me."

∼

Douglas MacNeil stood around six-foot-one, in a cotton shirt and tie, with tweed trousers, and a matching jacket over his arm. His short brown hair was greying at the temples and in a streak down the back. He had pushed his reading glasses atop his head, and had the confident, indulgent air one might expect from a general practitioner. The doctor's question about the DI's well-being made McKenzie feel like a patient.

"I'm very well," he answered. "Thank you for coming in, Dr MacNeil." He pointed him to a chair on the opposite side of the table. "I know this has been a difficult time for you and your friends."

The GP nodded. "We're helping each other through as best we can, but it's not been easy for any of us. I keep praying that nothing else happens."

"I understand you received a threatening letter a few weeks before Caitlin's murder?"

"Yes, that's right. We all did. Caitlin, Ewan, Isla, Finlay, and myself."

"Do you have the letter with you?"

"I do." MacNeil nodded, feeling his jacket pocket before fishing it out and handing it to the DI.

"We would like to hang on to this, Doctor."

"You can call me Douglas if you like." MacNeil pointed to the letter. "By all means, keep it. I didn't really know what to make of it at first. These letters came out of the blue. Now, they have sinister connotations, don't they? Likely, the author was deadly serious. But we took them for a troll, initially. We brushed it off."

The DI put on his reading glasses to examine the note. Except for one or two words, it was a carbon copy of the one sent to Isla. McKenzie frowned. "Are they all the same?" he asked.

"The letters?"

"Aye... I read Isla's yesterday, and this is virtually word for word."

MacNeil nodded. "They are pretty much all the same, yes. Same threats; same sentiment."

"But the sender doesn't say what you are supposed to have done to offend them."

The GP shrugged. "That's right, and it's why we didn't take it too seriously, at first. I mean, what offence could we possibly have committed as a group to make someone so angry? We assumed our limited success was the issue, and this was a jealous soul. But, honestly? We've been going over and over this since Caitlin and Ewan's death, wondering what the hell we could have done, and getting nowhere. Clearly, we are dealing with a psychopath. Someone with whom there is no reasoning."

"You think the author of this letter killed your friends?"

"Well, don't you?" MacNeil frowned, as though he couldn't see how the DI could view it otherwise. "People don't normally get this sort of mail, do they?"

"No, but letters like this rarely end in actual murder. You should always report them, of course, but often these are angry people letting off steam; punishing others by making them afraid. Reporting these threats and having police visit the sender makes them change their tune pretty quickly."

"I know." MacNeil ran a hand through his hair. "We should have come to you with these letters weeks ago. Caitlin hesitated to report them, while Isla dismissed them altogether, convinced a disgruntled troll was the sender."

"But you didn't agree?"

"I thought we should tell police right away. I thought it risky to ignore them."

"You thought right."

"So, what do we do now?"

"We will investigate the letters. Do you have the envelope? Were they posted to you or hand delivered?"

"They were posted. I have the envelope." He felt his pockets again. "Here." He handed over the folded envelope. It had a typed address and a second class stamp.

The DI screwed his eyes up as he tried to make out the postmark. "I'll get our forensic lab onto it. We should be able to locate the postbox, and there may be CCTV footage of the sender. There may even be DNA, if we are lucky."

MacNeil nodded. "That's good to know. I would feel safer knowing you'd caught this person."

"Who has handled this letter, Douglas?"

"Myself, Isla... er... probably all of us, actually. We took them to dinner one night and compared them. If I remember rightly, we all touched the letters."

"I see. Well, we will need DNA samples from your group, and anyone else who handled them, so we can extract your profiles and see if we have the sender's DNA. That won't be a problem, will it?"

"Er, no... Of course not."

"Good, we'll arrange for the samples to be taken when convenient for you. A simple mouth swab should be sufficient."

"I can do mine today, if you wish."

"That would be very helpful, Dr MacNeil, thank you. I will ask an officer to do a buccal swab on your way out."

"Very well."

"Is there anything else concerning you at the moment?" McKenzie cocked his head. "It can't have been easy, losing two of your friends like that. We will increase patrols around your home address and the surgery."

"That's reassuring." The GP thought for a moment. "Caitlin was a wonderful soul, Inspector. There were few like her."

"I understand you two were close, and you had known each other since early childhood?"

"That's right. She has been one of my best friends for as long as I can remember. We were toddlers together. I don't recall a time when she wasn't in my life... until now." His eyes fell to the table as though he were seeing her in his mind's eye.

"You knew her as well as anyone." McKenzie regarded him, head still cocked.

MacNeil nodded. "I would say so, although we were not

as close in later years. Oh, we were still the best of friends, but our lives pulled us in different directions. We met for dinner and parties as a group, but we didn't see as much of each other. Funny..." he gave a wry smile. "There was a time when I imagined we would spend the rest of our lives together."

"I understand you dated in high school?"

"We did. But we were heading to different universities and agreed a long distance relationship probably wouldn't work. I fell in love with someone else on my course, and got married the year before graduation."

"This was the lady who left-" McKenzie paused, wondering if this was insensitive.

The GP's eyes flicked up to his. "Who left to be with someone else, yes." He sighed. "I was working as a resident doctor at University College Hospital in London, and my time was not my own. We barely saw each other much of the time. I often had to sleep at the hospital because of working very long hours. I guess she became bored, and her head turned elsewhere."

"Where is she now?"

MacNeil shrugged. "I don't know. She disappeared. Miranda never told me where she was going, or who with. She simply up and left one day while I was at work. I never heard from her again."

"I see." McKenzie felt for him. "And you didn't rekindle it with Caitlin?"

He shook his head. "It wouldn't have been right. And, besides, I was still grieving the loss of my wife. I met someone else a few years ago. Katie is my rock."

"How much did you know about Caitlin's coffee company?"

"I knew coffee was her passion, and that she travelled a

lot to source product, and meet wholesale customers. She loved the cut and thrust of business. She was very good at it, and great with people."

"Was there any reason she might want to hide who she was on some of these trips? Maybe because she was visiting dangerous areas of the world?"

MacNeil frowned. "I don't understand."

"She discussed nothing like that with you?"

"No. I didn't think she needed to hide who she was."

"Have you any idea who might have wanted to hurt Caitlin or Ewan? Anyone besides the unknown author of the letters? Did either of them tell you about anyone causing difficulties, or following them? Acting strange?"

"Not that I can recall, Inspector."

"And what about you?"

"Me?" His eyes widened.

"Yes, is anybody causing you concern for your safety who may or may not be the letter writer?"

"Not that I can think of, no."

"If you have such worries going forward, I'd like you to let us know right away."

"I will."

"I guess that will be all for now, Doctor MacNeil. McKenzie got up to show him to reception. We'll take that swab on your way out."

∼

SANDY-HAIRED AND STUBBLED, Finlay Scott arrived ten minutes early for his interview. Small in stature, but wiry, he had sweat on his upper lip, and flicked nervous glances around reception.

Dalgleish showed him to the interview room, where he

draped his jacket over the back of the chair before sitting. The DC took a seat opposite; making small talk as they waited for McKenzie to join them.

"Sorry to keep you waiting," the DI said, as he placed a file and loose papers down on the table. He held out his hand. "Grant McKenzie, MIT."

Scott shook it, his hand cold and clammy. "Finlay Scott."

The DI resisted wiping his hand on his trouser leg. "You're an English teacher at a secondary school?" he asked, reading from his notes.

"That's right. I've been a teacher for nine years."

"Enjoy it?"

"It has its moments..."

"And you received a threatening letter from an unknown person?"

"I did." Scott opened a leather document wallet he had brought with him, fishing out the letter still in its envelope. "There you go."

"When did you receive it?" McKenzie donned nitrile gloves before accepting the missive; opening it to read the contents.

"A few weeks before... before the murders."

"How did it make you feel?"

"Worried; frightened, even. No one had ever sent me anything like this before."

"Were you surprised to learn all of your friends also received a copy?"

"I was. And I was somewhat relieved to realise I wasn't alone. But it was still unsettling."

"It would be." McKenzie nodded. "Did you not consider taking this letter to police?"

"We thought about it. I mean myself and my friends. We were unsure how seriously we should take it. Isla thought it the work of a jealous troll. Because of her, I felt calmer about it. She really knows how to make someone feel better. She's amazing, actually."

"And Caitlin and Ewan were your friends, too?"

"Yes, we often met as a group, Isla, myself, Caitlin, Ewan, and Douglas. I would usually book the dinner table, often at The Dome here in Edinburgh, and we met at least once a month to catch up on each other's lives."

"Did any of you meet outside of those dinners?"

"I play squash regularly with Douglas. Usually at least twice a month. Ewan used to play squash with us, too. And we went to the occasional party for birthdays and Christmas, that sort of thing."

"Did you meet any of the ladies for sports matches or drinks?"

"No. I've asked Isla out a few times, but she never accepts. She is always busy, busy, busy."

"You like her?"

Finlay coloured. "She's a lovely lass."

"And what about Caitlin?"

"Caitlin always focused on her business, and she was often deep in thought, even at our dinners. Her eyes would glaze over, and I would wonder where she had gone to in her head. She took frequent trips abroad and sometimes missed our dinners. But she came to them whenever she was in the country. She was going places; you know? Her business was going from strength to strength. The killer robbed her of that. And Ewan… He wasn't a high-flyer like Caitlin or Isla, but he knew what he wanted, and was growing in confidence. The new shops would have been a colossal success, I've no doubt. God only knows what will happen to all that now." The teacher shuddered. "And what if the killer doesn't stop there? What if he really is the nutcase who wrote these letters? We none of us are safe, Inspector."

"I understand your nervousness, Mr Scott. And we have increased patrols around your homes and places of work. What I would suggest to all of you is that you do not go anywhere on foot, alone after dark or before the sun comes up. Be sensible, and aware of your surroundings. Should anything cause you concern, or if you receive any more of these letters, let us know immediately. We can look at extra security for your homes. But increased, highly visible patrols should suffice for now. Caitlin and Ewan died in Edinburgh parks. I would suggest not going to open spaces, especially not on your own. Going as part of a larger group in the middle of the day may be safest."

"Aye, understood. That's what I was planning, anyway. I shudder to think of the killer hiding out in parks, waiting for us."

"If the perpetrator is targeting members of your group specifically, they are unlikely to be waiting around on the off chance one of you shows up. They will have followed Caitlin and Ewan and learned their routines. Or, they followed them in the hours before they attacked them. Of course, we don't know for sure your group is being targeted. But I admit it looks that way, especially given the letters. It could also simply be a horrible coincidence that a psychopathic serial killer, hunting strangers, *murder*ed two of your friends. Someone who hangs around in parks looking for victims. Either way, avoiding those areas would minimise your risk. We have warning posters going up around the city, and news conferences to inform the public. In the meantime, Mr Scott, I suggest you remain vigilant."

"I will."

"We will need a mouth swab from you, for DNA, if that

is okay? We'll examine the letters for evidence of the perpetrator and need to rule out your genetic material and prints."

Finlay nodded. "Of course, I understand."

"Good. Is there anything else you would like to tell me?"

Scott shook his head. "Nothing that comes to mind at the moment."

"Then that will be all for today. We will probably speak to you again as our investigation progresses. In the meantime, here is our contact number." He pushed a card across the desk. "Call us if there is anything further you think we should know or if you have any other concerns."

"Thanks." He put the card in a zip pocket of the document wallet.

"Detective Constable Dalgleish will see you out."

"One last thing..." Finlay turned back just before he reached the door.

"Go on..."

"Isla..."

"What about her?"

"You have patrols looking out for her, right?"

"Yes, we have them looking out for you all."

"I couldn't bear for anything to happen to her."

"Aye." McKenzie grinned. "I can see that. I think you have a sweet spot for our Ms Campbell, eh?"

Scott coloured again. "Just so long as she's safe, Inspector."

∽

"So, he's got the hots for Isla, eh? I would have had him down as gay." Dalgleish flicked his head. "He's a wee bit effeminate, do you not think?"

"Maybe." The DI pulled a face. "Or maybe it's his small stature and tiny hands you're thinking of?"

"Ach, could be. I'll get the letters off to forensics this afternoon. We should have the profiles by the end of the week."

"Good. The sooner the better."

9

ROCK OF DEATH

"Here we are again, Grant." Fiona donned nitrile gloves from a box on the side.

"Aye..." McKenzie grimaced. "Another poor sod hit on the head when he was only out for a walk."

"It was a bit out of the way this time, wasn't it?" She adjusted her glasses and pulled back the sheet covering Ewan McDonald's body.

"Away at Duddingston Loch. It's a beautiful place, but I don't know why he was walking amid the trees near the Kirk. There were visitors not that far away, but the tearooms were closed. The trees are a fairly secluded area."

"Could he have been visiting the kirk? Maybe to find solace after losing one of his friends?"

"That could be the reason. It's certainly a beautiful spot to remember Caitlin, but he couldn't have lit a candle in remembrance because the kirk wasn't open. Only the grounds were accessible, and Dr Neil's Garden where volunteers were working. I'll be heading over there later to look around again, and speak to the someone at the kirk. Nobody saw or heard anything at the time of the murder, though. And the killer tossed the weapon into the lake."

"Don't tell me, another stone?"

"Aye, and a fair-sized one."

"I expected as much, looking at these head injuries. A large angular stone with sharp edges likely made these wounds. The killer must be reasonably strong, I would say. I need to see that rock."

"It should be on its way over. Forensics are all but finished with it. Unfortunately, the water washed away much of the evidence. The killer didn't mess about, did he?"

Fiona shook her head. "I doubt the victim saw it coming. There are no defensive wounds. Not even bruises to the hands and arms from the fall. The first blow likely killed him outright."

"The victim's friends are all nervous. I can't say I blame them. Someone sent them threatening letters, and now two of them are dead. That's enough to put the wind up anyone."

"I bet they're scared witless."

"I've seen the letters. The lab is analysing them as we speak."

"So you don't think this killer is going to stop?"

"That's my fear. We have to find him before anyone else gets hurt."

Fiona cast her eyes over the victim. "Such a waste. Another victim barely in their thirties."

"And another thriving local business cut short. And we still can't be sure of the motive. There are a few skeletons in these closets, though, I can tell you."

"Well, good luck with all that." She cocked her head. "You'll find the perp. I have every faith in you."

"Thanks." He gave a wry smile. "I'm glad *you* have."

A BONE chilling mist hovered over Duddingston Loch, although the sun shone on the wildlife haven. Snow from the previous day had all but melted away, leaving only a few clumps here and there, clinging to the grasses along the paths and the water's edge. McKenzie and Dalgleish made their way through the trees towards the water.

"The killer would have emerged from somewhere around there." Dalgleish pointed to an area spanning a few yards in front of the trees. "They found the stone in the loch. He'd have had to go pretty close to toss it, too. A rock of that weight would be hard to throw far, and divers found it three metres out — probably thrown like a shot-put."

"Where did he get the rock from?" McKenzie frowned.

"He took it from the dry-stone wall back there. I asked the garden volunteers if they had noticed any missing, and they showed me a gap. The murder weapon looked like it came from the wall. Same stone. Over the years, people dug a few from the ground, but this one had the same shape as the others in the wall. The extended garden surrounds this area here and goes off to the left." He pointed beyond the trees. "It wouldn't have been difficult for perp to hide one amongst the trees before the murder."

"Except he wouldn't have known Ewan would come down here, would he?"

"Not unless he asked to meet him? Or otherwise found out he was coming."

"If the killer knew Ewan was coming, it suggests he had access to Ewan or his contacts... Maybe he talked to them?"

"Or he could have followed them on social media. I've been looking at the group's accounts and, as you would expect of a lot of young people today, they were updating fairly regularly. Caitlin's posts were mostly about her travels, coffee, and fair trade practices. Ewan divided his posts between cafe announcements, photos of happy customers, and personal updates like nights out. If Ewan suggested on a post that he might go down to Duddingston loch. It's possible the killer saw that and prepared accordingly."

"We need to know whether he told others he would be here."

Dalgleish nodded. "I'll check for it when I get back."

McKenzie turned back towards the trees. "So maybe the killer knew Ewan would be here, and lay in wait. But he still wouldn't know when he would arrive. That's a lot of faffing around."

"Murder is a lot of faffing around, Grant. If the killer wanted it badly enough..."

"Aye, you're right."

"And we know this perp was so angry with this group he sent them death threats. That shows a high level of motivation for evil, right there."

"Maybe the killer invited Ewan here." The DI pressed his lips together as he cast his gaze around the trees.

"It's possible Caitlin and Ewan knew their killer," Dalgleish agreed.

"The problem is, they knew many people through their businesses. We'll need a wide net to catch this perp."

"Inspector? Inspector McKenzie?" The gravelly voice was quickly followed by a grey-haired; shaggy-bearded gentleman in a raincoat, woollen hat, and wellingtons.

Grant and Graham turned to greet him.

"Doddy Gray," the man announced, stopping to catch his breath. "They said I'd find you out this way."

"Doddy Gray?" McKenzie shook the man's hand. "I'm sorry, I don't know who-"

"I volunteer in the garden." He paused, looking towards the water. "I found him…"

"I see." The DI estimated Gray to be around sixty years old. "It must have given you a fright?"

"It did. I was fair shocked, I can tell you. I wasn't expecting that when I sat down on the bench to eat my sandwiches. There was a leg and foot sticking out from the trees, near to the water's edge. I thought at first it might be a drunk laying down for a nap. I was going to give them short shrift, I can tell you. But when I got there, I saw that his head and shoulders were covered in blood. I threw up."

"What time was that?"

"About eleven -thirty in the morning. They said he'd most likely been there overnight."

"Did you see anyone else around, Mr Gray?"

"Only in the garden and in the kirk grounds. A few visitors out for a stroll. There was no-one down this way. I often sit by the water to eat my food. Sometimes people walk down here, but it was quiet that morning."

"Did you know the victim?"

"I couldn't make out his features with all the blood, and I didn't stop to examine him. I ran back to get my phone from my bag and call the police. My fingers could barely press the right keys. I was shaking from head to toe. I still don't feel right."

"The victim's name was Ewan MacDonald. Does that ring any bells?"

"Ewan MacDonald…" Gray screwed his face up. "It sounds kind of familiar…"

"He ran a coffee Shop on Cockburn Street."

"I knew I recognised the name. Yes, I know the coffee shop, though I've only been in there a few times with my daughter. Nice man." His eyes glazed over. "What a horrible way to go."

"Did you notice any vehicles hanging around, Doddy? Anything that struck you as unusual at the kirk?"

"There were a few cars parked up that day. I assumed they belonged to walkers. The dead man's vehicle was abandoned in the car park. It's still there, with police tape all around it. I can't say that I noticed any cars that stood out. Do you have a particular vehicle in mind? We get all sorts up here, aside from regulars like, the volunteers... I would recognise their cars."

"A black Lexus?"

"A black Lexus... No, I can't say I noticed one of those. But I didn't go looking at every car in the car park. I wasn't minded to before I found the body, and I was too shook afterwards to go looking. I just let the police officers get on with it, and went home early, after I'd given my statement, of course."

"Was the kirk open?"

Gray shook his head. "Och, no. They lock the kirk when not in use, and the tearoom is not open for visitors during the winter. They will be open again in the spring."

"Is there anything else you can tell us, Mr Gray?"

"I can't think of anything at the moment."

"Give us a ring, if you do." McKenzie felt in his coat pocket, fishing out a dog-eared card. "Call us on that number if you think of anything or if you see anyone up here acting suspiciously."

"Aye, all right, Inspector."

As they made their way back to the car, Grant tapped Dalgleish on the shoulder. "There it is again, look..."

Graham squinted at a dark car some distance away. "You think that's the same one? I canna tell if it's a Lexus."

McKenzie pulled a face. "I think maybe I'm losing it. I'm seeing them everywhere now."

Dalgleish laughed. "I think you need time out."

10

GHOSTS OF THE LOST

Back at the MIT office, Grant approached Helen McAllister as she tapped her keyboard, peering at images on the screen. "Any luck with finding CCTV of the letter sender?" he asked, pulling up a chair.

"Mixed news, I'm afraid." She grimaced, sitting back in her chair and rubbing her eyes. "The lab came up trumps. They confirmed the letters were posted in Linlithgow," she said, referring to a village nineteen miles out of Edinburgh. "And we have a rough timeframe to work to. But someone has already recorded over the CCTV footage we could have accessed. If only they had come to us about the letters sooner."

"Aye, I ken..." The DI sighed. "Is there any chance of us getting anything at all?"

"We've a couple more places to contact, so I haven't lost all hope, but it's looking unlikely we'll get much."

"Thank you for this, Helen, but keep at it until we've exhausted all possibilities. And get yourself a coffee. Your eyes are looking sore."

"Thanks. How did it go at the kirk?" she asked.

"We know where the rock came from that was used to kill Ewan MacDonald. But we got little else. Let's hope forensics yields something. I swear I saw that Lexus again, though. It was too far away to be sure, but I've got an uncanny feeling I'm being followed."

"You think it's the killer?"

"I don't know… But I think someone is taking a very keen interest in our investigation. And I would really like to know who. Though I am worried I'm getting a wee bit paranoid about it."

"Just don't get yourself bashed over the head, eh?" She grinned at him. "Maybe you better wear a crash helmet around the place."

He laughed. "Can you imagine? Everybody would ask me where I'd stashed my bike." He stood. "Can you do me a favour after you've had a break?"

"Sure." She nodded.

"Can you check the Corstophine Woods crime scene footage and CCTV again? Look for any sign of a black Lexus. There's no rush for that. Finish whatever else you need to do first, and I don't need the results today. I'm going to delve into the background of Caitlin, Ewan, and their friends to see if anything jumps out at me. The killer had to have either known Caitlin and Ewan, or stalked them prior to killing them. He knew where they would be and when. I want to know what it is about them and their friends that made him target them like this. We know Caitlin was likely being followed by the intelligence services. If she was working for smugglers, and something went wrong, they may have silenced her. But how would that link with Ewan? And why were her friends sent those letters? Graham was going to trawl through their social media to see if the killer was stalking them online. I'm going to see what I can dig up regarding known smuggling operations."

"Aye, I can check the footage for you after I've made the brew. Would you like one?"

"I wouldna say no." He grinned. "Is Sinclair about?"

"He's in his office. He asked where you were earlier. I told him you were checking out the crime scene in King's Park."

"Thanks, Helen. I'll catch up with him later."

∼

"Have you got a minute?" Dalgleish called to the DI as he made his way across the office.

"Aye, what have you got?"

Graham grimaced. "Not a lot, I'm afraid."

"Oh..."

"I have trawled all of Ewan's available social media posts, and I can't find any reference to his trip to Duddingston. Not even one line. As far as I can see, he didn't make his intention to go there public, nor did he tell anyone on social media he was there."

"What about direct messages?"

"He didn't send any that day. Not a one. Most of his social media activity for the last several weeks had been about his coffee shops, and the excitement of starting two new ones."

McKenzie frowned. "Are there any that mentioned Caitlin Murray?"

"Aye, she was at one of the cafe opening ceremonies. There are a few photographs of them smiling and hugging and looking proud of his achievements." Dalgleish sighed. "She looked so happy, Grant. So did he. It's hard seeing that, knowing they are both dead. They had it all to look forward to."

"Could they have been an item? Perhaps they were becoming more than friends. Maybe someone couldn't take that? The ex-boyfriend, perhaps?"

"There's nothing in the profiles to suggest they were seeing each other. Nothing to say they were lovers or dating. As far as I can see, Ewan had dated a few girls, but nothing that was serious. I guess his focus was on his business."

"So, if he didn't post on social media about visiting Duddingston Loch, it suggests he may have told his killer in person."

"Unless the killer was lying in wait for any victim that happened his way."

"That makes no sense, Graham. What are the chances of a serial killer, picking parks at random, murdering two friends that had recently received threatening letters?"

"Well, when you put it like that..."

"Exactly. Ewan almost certainly knew his killer. And perhaps Caitlin did too."

"So we look for mutual acquaintances."

"I think we have to, and cross-link with those of the other friends. There will be someone in common with all five of them."

"Ewan's sister has been in touch." Dalgliesh scratched his head. "She'd like to speak with us. She said she could meet us at his flat above the shop in Cockburn Street. Our forensics guys have finished with it, but it would give us a chance to look around and get some intel from his family. She said her name was Sarah, and she'll be sorting his things to save her parents the pain of doing it."

"Aye, all right. Let me know when she can meet, and we'll be there."

∼

THE RAIN HAD HELD OFF, but the air was thick with a grey chill that matched the mood of the gathering. McKenzie stood a respectful distance behind the cluster of mourners, beyond the shadows of the old yew tree looming over the gravesite. He could see the family, their stoic faces streaked with grief; holding onto each other and taking turns to throw a rose onto Caitlin Murray's coffin as it was slowly lowered into the cold earth.

The vicar's words drifted through the damp air with a cadence that spoke of eternal rest and the promise of peace everlasting. As McKenzie caught fragments of it, "... ashes to ashes, dust to dust...", his eyes were no longer on the mourners, but on the trees lining the field next to the main road.

The case gnawed at him. Were Caitlin and Ewan tied together by more than shared interests and their subsequent murder? The killer must have known them, he was certain of that. The question was, how well?

The DI shifted his weight, crossing his arms against the cold. He thought of Caitlin's enigmatic life, the unexplained bank transactions, and multiple passports. What had this, if anything, to do with Ewan? And what was the thread that connected them to the murderer who had ended their young lives with such brutality?

A flicker of motion caught his eye, beyond the sparse line of skeletal trees framing the cemetery. A black Lexus crawled by, its polished surface catching the dim afternoon light like a lingering shadow. McKenzie's stomach knotted. How many times had he seen that car? Three? Four? More? He had lost count.

Was it even the same one? Or was he imagining things?

The make and model were not exactly rare, and yet something about it and the way it drove by like a ghost made him swallow hard.

He squinted, trying to make out the driver through the glare on the windows without success. The vehicle rolled on, disappearing beyond the curve of the road.

His jaw clenched. Was it the killer come to gloat over Caitlin's burial? Or was he losing his grip, seeing suspicious activity where there was none? The case was getting under his skin. He even dreamed about that damn car, always just out of reach, its driver faceless, taunting.

A hand brushed his coat as someone from the gathered mourners stumbled, their face blotchy and raw with tears. McKenzie muttered an apology and stepped further back, his reverie over the car broken. He checked his watch, noting the time. With any luck, they could pull CCTV from a nearby camera and have a registration for the car he had just witnessed — innocent or not.

The vicar's voice grew faint in his ears as he reached into his pocket for his notebook and jotted down the time and a brief description. It wasn't much, but it was something.

As the family began drifting away, Caitlin's mum whispered words over the grave. McKenzie lingered to watch, knowing the pain she must be in. He would talk to her and Caitlin's father again, but now was not the time. His eyes returned to the road. He'd check with the others later, to see if anyone else had reported seeing a car like that near Ewan's shop before he died. He couldn't shake the feeling that he wasn't being paranoid.

That black Lexus might be nothing. Or it could be everything.

11

STRANGE

Although Grant had desperately hoped they could pull CCTV with the Lexus' numberplate from cameras near the kirkyard, he was going to be disappointed.

Graham took a deep breath before delivering the bad news.

"Did you get it?" McKenzie asked, crossing the room.

"Aye, we've got footage from the only camera in the vicinity, but I warn you now, you won't be happy."

"Why, what's the matter?"

"Come and see for yourself." Dalgleish ran a hand through his hair, frustration creasing his forehead. "I canna understand it, sir. I mean, the car is right there, but there's a glare or something interfering with the image. And we just can't get it any clearer. The lab got back to me a couple of minutes ago, and they've had no luck either."

Grant peered at Dalgleish's screen, squinting as though it would make a difference. Graham was right. Diagonal streaks of light obscured the car's driver and registration. "What the hell caused that?" He gave a guttural groan. "Of all the bloody luck... I was pinning my hopes on that damn camera."

"It's odd..." Dalgleish pushed his hands deep into his pockets. "I don't understand where the glare came from. I mean, it isn't as though it was in strong sunlight. It's dull as ditch water out there. Another vehicle's lights must have blinded the camera. It's the only explanation I can come up with, unless there is a fault with the lens. But if we move the video further along, you can see the following cars fine, both driver and numberplate. Everything is crystal clear."

"I tell you, Graham, that Lexus gives me the creeps."

"There's something else that bothers me about this..." Dalgleish blew air through pursed lips, still staring at his screen. "It's not just glare, Grant. Look at the edges... It's too clean; like someone deliberately scrambled the signal. Normal footage doesn't glitch like this. Maybe, if this is a criminal gang, they're using jamming technology to obscure themselves. They'd have to be a pretty high-end outfit to have all that going on, though. We're talking a serious drug or people smuggling racket."

"Aye, well, I've been thinking along those lines, anyway. Whatever Caitlin got herself mixed up in, it was clearly pretty serious, and likely resulted in her death. And, since her business was linked to Ewan, that might explain why someone targeted him, too. If this is a gang, they don't mess about. Any idea what they might use to obscure the image like that?"

The DC shrugged. "Infrared light emitters, maybe? Cloaking systems? Or other jamming equipment? I'm afraid I'm not too up on all that. I know it exists. That's about it. We could ask folks at the lab. They'll have more of an idea than I do. We can get them on the case."

"You think they could unscramble it for us?"

"We can ask."

The DI sighed as he moved away from the screen. "If there is a serious smuggling ring on our patch, I want them off it and in jail where they belong. But we'll need to watch our backs. They'll attempt to get rid of anyone in their way, including police officers. I don't want any of us at risk, but we will get Caitlin and Ewan's killers. Whatever it takes."

∽

THE DOOR to Ewan's flat above his coffee shop on Cockburn Street creaked open. The air inside was cold and damp. Someone had left a sash window open an inch to let in air. But it was frightening how fast an old building could deteriorate when left unoccupied.

The open-plan lounge area was tidy, but not obsessively so. The mug last used by Ewan sat on the low coffee table, complete with separated dregs of tea or perhaps coffee in the bottom. A crime scene officer had evidently dusted it for fingerprints. Their report had noted nothing remarkable about the victim's home. There was no evidence the killer had met Ewan there.

A side cupboard held an old stereo and a rack of CDs, many of which appeared older than their owner had been. A couple of books about business lay on the floor next to the couch. Perhaps Ewan had flicked through them the night before his fateful trip to Duddingston Loch.

Grant crossed to the alcove next to a bricked-up fireplace, running his eyes over the spines of the books housed on its shelving.

"Ewan's sister will be here soon," Dalgleish looked through the window at the street outside; closing it to keep out the cold for a while.

"When's she due?" McKenzie turned to him.

"She'll be here in about ten minutes, depending on traffic."

"No problem. I'll look at the other rooms."

The small bathroom contained a toilet and shower, only. The DI opened a tall metal cabinet and found toiletries, a toothbrush, a comb, and a yellowing picture of a couple with two children and a dog. McKenzie guessed the children were Ewan and his younger sister, Anne. He swallowed, turning for the bedroom.

A can of deodorant sat alongside a bottle of aftershave on the bedroom cupboard. He removed the lid and inhaled; it wasn't Ralph Loren. This was not the scent he had detected in Caitlin's walk-in wardrobe.

In a basket at the foot of the bed, near the window, lay a crumpled shirt, trousers and other items, presumably intended for a wash that would no longer take place. And in the corner, an old wardrobe with clothes still hanging inside. But there was little else to speak of the life Ewan led, and no notebooks or diaries to suggest why he went to Duddingston that day.

"She's here," Dalgleish called from the lounge.

McKenzie heard a key turning in the lock and headed back to greet Ewan's younger sibling.

"Sorry I'm late." She stashed a soaking umbrella in the corner and pulled the hood of her raincoat off her head, revealing curly blonde hair. "I'm Annie MacDonald," she said, offering her hand to Dalgleish, shrewd blue eyes appraising the detectives.

"DC Graham Dalgleish," he answered, shaking the offered hand. "And this here is DI Grant McKenzie. He's the man in charge of investigating your brother's murder."

She nodded. "It was a helluva shock to us, as you can

imagine." She unzipped her raincoat before taking it off and draping it over the cold radiator. "My parents are distraught. I'm dealing with his estate because they couldn't cope with it just now. Their heads are all over the place. My mam hasn't stopped crying since she was told."

"It must be devastating for you all," Grant agreed. "I can't blame them for not feeling able to deal with his belongings. They, and you, will need time to come to terms with what's happened."

"I spoke with him over the phone, only the other day. He was so happy about the new shops he was opening. He was absolutely full of it. I don't think I'd ever heard him so excited." She looked away towards the window over the street. "It's so hard to accept that he is gone."

"Do you have someone to help you with all this?" McKenzie imagined she, too, might feel overwhelmed, sorting it all on top of the grief of her brother's loss.

"Not really... My partner works shifts as a paramedic. Don't get me wrong, he does what he can, but I can't expect him to be here going through all this with me. My employer gave me a couple of weeks off work as compassionate leave. I work part time for a supermarket... Asda." She sighed, casting her eyes around the flat. "I'm not really sure what to do with it all."

The DI pushed his hands deep into his trouser pockets. He wondered if Annie's thin frame could move boxes full of stuff around. But, in sweatshirt and jogging bottoms, she appeared to have dressed for it. "What will you do with his things?" he asked.

"We'll sell some of it to help pay for his funeral. He didn't have life insurance or anything like that. I guess he didn't think he'd need it being so young. The family will keep items that were special to him."

"And the shops?"

"We're not sure, yet." She rubbed her forehead. "He owned this flat and the shop below. The two new premises were rented, but he owned all the equipment and stock. There'll be wages to pay for the staff, too. Everything has stopped for the moment and, to be honest, I don't have a clue about coffee. I enjoy a cup, that's about it. John, that's my partner, thinks it best we sell the business as a going concern. This flat and the shop should be part of that sale. We hope to find a buyer quickly."

"Shall we sit somewhere comfortable?" Grant waited for Annie to seat herself on the couch. "You are a few years younger than Ewan?"

"Aye, six years. He turned thirty-five in April of this year."

"And he didn't have a wife? A partner?"

She shook her head. "He was engaged a few years back. But when it fell through, he sold the ring to John." She held up her left hand, showing a round diamond set in what appeared to be a platinum ring.

The DI balked at how matter-of-factly she showed it off. He swallowed. "How did you hear about Ewan's death?"

Her eyes glazed over. "I was getting ready for work when the call came through to our home in Corstophine. I didn't think it was real at first. They must have mistaken him for someone else, I thought. Then it sank in that it really was him. And… and I couldn't believe it. Especially since one of his best friends was found dead in the woods by us not so long ago. I mean, what are the chances?"

"Aye, exactly. We believe the murders are connected."

Her eyes met his. He could almost see the wheels turning. And, although he was well aware people deal with grief differently, Annie MacDonald appeared surprisingly unscathed. Oh, there were the beginnings of bags under those shrewd blue eyes, but there was no evidence she'd been crying. That was unusual amongst the relatives he had spoken to in the past, unless there had been a family strife or rift. "How well did you get on with Ewan?" he asked, head cocked.

"We got on well enough." Her eyes narrowed. "Why are you asking me that?"

"Did you see him much?"

"Once or twice a month, maybe? You know what it's like with busy lives. And Ewan was always working."

"Did you see him at the coffee shop?"

"Aye, I've been there a few times over the last few years. I prefer tea, mind, and I'm nae bothered about fancy coffee, either. I drink instant mostly when I have it. But I went along when Ewan had his opening, and I had been a few times since."

"What were you like growing up together?"

"We were okay when I was little. But Ewan, being so much older than me, he preferred playing with bigger kids once he got to a certain age. I don't blame him. That's just what kids are like. We had our own friends, you know?"

"When was the last time you saw your brother?"

"Um..." She turned her eyes towards the ceiling. "That would have been about a month ago. He popped round to see mam and dad, and I was there at the same time. That's usually how we ended up seeing each other. We'd catch up on the phone sometimes, if it had been a while. That's how it is for most people, isn't it? I mean, life kinda gets in the way a bit."

"How did you feel when you learned about his death?"

"I was horrified." She cast her eyes downward. "Like I said, I couldn't believe it. And then, when I heard someone had bopped him over the head, I was shocked to the core. Who would do such a thing? And to my big brother? John was all for castrating the culprit."

"John, your partner?"

"Aye."

"Have you any idea who could have attacked Ewan like that?"

"Well, you know, I've wracked my brains for days over that. I mean, Ewan and I have had our differences over the years, but he was a good man with a lot of friends. He was easy-going. You have to be good with people in the business he was in. I honestly think Ewan must have been in the wrong place at the wrong time. I think it had to have been a killer who just wanted to murder someone that day."

"And Caitlin?" McKenzie watched Annie's eyes. They never flickered.

"Aye, well, that's a helluva coincidence, right enough." She stopped talking, pursing her lips.

"Did Ewan mention being concerned about anyone, to either you or your parents? Or of being afraid of someone?"

"Not that I remember, no. I can't even recall him disagreeing with anyone. But then, he must have met a lot of folks doing the job he did. Maybe one of them had a problem with him. I can't think why they would, but there's nowt as crazy as folks, is there?"

"What will happen to the proceeds when the business is sold?"

"At the moment, it's looking like John and I will get whatever's left after taxes. Mam and dad want nothing to do with all that. Mam says she wouldn't want to get any of the money. It'd be too much like benefitting from his death. Blood money, she calls it."

"And what did you say to her when she said that?"

"I told her it has to go somewhere. Ewan wasn't married, and didn't leave any heirs. The proceeds would all go to the government if we didn't accept it. And I can tell you now, my brother wouldn't have wanted that."

"No, I guess he wouldn't." Grant wasn't sure what to make of Annie. She was practical, he could see that, but was there more to this and her lack of obvious emotion? "When is the funeral?"

"It's looking like next Wednesday. We are waiting to confirm with the undertaker. We're trying to get a plot near his friend's grave."

"Whose, Caitlin's?"

She looked towards the window again. "Aye... They said we could have one not too far away. I have to go there tomorrow afternoon to look around and arrange it."

"It's good of you to sort everything for your parents."

"Mam hasn't wanted to get out of bed. Oh, she gets up," she added. "But dad has to coax her. It's taken a toll on him, too. He looks a lot older all of a sudden."

"Death has that effect."

"For me, too. It's still sinking in, Inspector. I keep thinking the phone will ring or I'll get a text. I keep expecting his name to pop up when the phone pings."

"As I said before, we believe the same killer attacked Caitlin and your brother. We think this person knew their routine, or was in regular contact with them. Ewan likely told the killer where he was going that day, and they waited for him."

"And Caitlin?" she asked, tilting her head.

"We can't be sure. But it's likely the perpetrator knew her routine too, as she ran that route most days before starting work — unless she was abroad."

"Aye, she went away a lot, if I remember rightly."

"She did."

"It could have been a customer."

"Sorry?" McKenzie narrowed his eyes, listening intently.

"Ewan was very chatty with his customers. Oh, he had staff working for him, right enough. But he was always getting involved in conversations with folks. He loved greeting people and getting them settled. It was really important to him for the customer to feel looked after. He liked the personal touch. The few times I stopped for coffee at the shop, I watched him chatting away to everyone. He liked a good gossip, did Ewan."

"Except this killer hurt Caitlin first, and I'm not sure how that links in with Ewan's customers. Oh, I'm not ruling that out..." He held up a hand. "I'm just struggling with the mechanics of it. I know they liaised regularly over trialling coffee beans from various parts of the world, but we're still trying to pin down the motive for their murders."

"There were rumours, you know." Annie's eyes glazed over again.

"What rumours?"

"That she was leading a double life. That there was something not quite right with her. I mean, I wasn't going to say anything to you because I don't know if it's relevant, but there were rumours she was up to no good."

"Can you elaborate?" Dalgleish had his notebook out.

Annie leaned forward on the couch. "Ewan once said there were things she wouldn't talk about. Some of her trips, that sort of thing. He said she would go away sometimes for weeks and weeks. And, when she came back, she was exhausted... and thin. He said she looked too thin, and dark under the eyes. But, after a two or three weeks of being home, she'd recover; become a healthy weight again."

"But she was buying coffee beans on these trips, wasn't

she?" McKenzie was not about to mention the passports at this stage.

"Oh, aye, she was… But Ewan often wondered if there was more to it."

"Did he ask her about these excursions?"

"Aye, but he said she would close the conversation down or change it to something else. I get the impression he never got to the bottom of it. Could be, she got involved with some bad people."

"What were you doing the day of your brother's murder?"

"I was at home on one of my non-working days."

"Was John with you?"

"No, John worked a long shift that day. The ambulances were flat out."

"Did you see anyone else?"

"Are you asking me if I have an alibi for my brother's murder?"

"I didn't want to put it like that."

She frowned. "Why would I have wanted to kill my own brother?"

"We look at everyone, Annie. You want us to do a thorough job, don't you? We owe Ewan that."

Her face softened. "Aye, all right. But I was washing and ironing for hours that afternoon. And I didn't see anyone. I heard the postman drop letters through the door, but I picked them up later on when the ironing was done, and he didn't see me. John was on the day shift, and he got home about seven that evening."

"I see."

"So, I've no alibi, but I didn't kill my brother. You need to spend your time finding the person who did." She looked at her watch. "I'm sorry, Inspector, but I've a lot to do just now."

"Of course." McKenzie rose from the couch.

Dalgleish put his notebook away.

"We'll leave you to it. Thanks for speaking to us today. We'll be in touch." Grant nodded to Graham, and they let themselves out of the flat.

∼

"Well, what do you make of her, then?" Graham pulled a face as they headed back along Cockburn Street towards their vehicle. "She's one cold cookie, eh?"

"She certainly seems unflappable," the DI agreed. "She's also dealing with her brother's death remarkably well, unlike her parents."

"Do you think there's more to it?"

"I think we should keep our eye on Annie and her partner. They may be innocent enough, but her responses were unusually cool regarding Ewan's brutal death. That doesn't make her guilty, but I think we should look into her."

"I'll do some digging when we get back."

12

ON EDGE

Back at his home in The Grange, among Edinburgh's leafy suburbs, Grant said goodnight to his children. Martha had fallen fast asleep after her tea and hadn't stirred when her father carried her upstairs. Craig yawned profusely but had not yet succumbed to sleep. Davie was awake and reading.

The DI smiled to himself. He didn't always get to say goodnight to them, so it wasn't something he ever took for granted. They wouldn't be this little forever. He was simply happy to be in the moment with them.

"All settled?" Jane asked as he quietly closed the lounge door.

"All settled." He grinned. "I think Davie may be awake for a while, though. He's having adventures with wands and wizards."

She nodded. "You know I caught him the other night still reading at two am, don't you? I don't know how he manages school after reading till that time, but he seems to."

"Ach, he's a bright boy. He needs a lot to occupy his

mind. I don't think he'll be awake long tonight. He'll be asleep soon enough."

"I'm getting tired myself." Jane flicked through the TV channels with the remote. "I'm not sure what to put on."

"I'll draw the curtains." Grant crossed the lounge to the bay window, pulling at the edges of the heavy material. The streetlights outside bathed everything in a pale amber glow, broken by the silhouette of a passing car as it streaked across the glass. As he pulled the fabric shut, another vehicle caught his eye, a sleek black Lexus idling at the curbside a few houses down.

His hand froze on the curtain, and blood began pounding in his ears, drowning out the muffled sound of the television. The car's polished surface gleamed in the lamplight. McKenzie swallowed. "How the hell did they get my address?" he muttered.

"Sorry?" his wife called from the couch.

He didn't stay to answer. Letting go of the curtain, he turned on his heel and ran for the door.

"Grant? What's the matter?"

"I'll be right back," he answered, his voice cracked.

"What have you seen?" she asked, her voice more urgent.

"I thought I saw something outside." He didn't wait for her reply as he ran to the front door without grabbing his jacket from the hall stand. The cold air hit him hard as he headed out, scanning the street as he flew down the path.

The Lexus pulled away, its engine cutting through the quiet night. Grant's heart thumped in his chest as he followed it, eyes narrowing to see if he could make out the driver through the back window. The tension in his chest had him fighting for breath.

The Lexus disappeared, its taillights vanishing down the street.

"Damn!" he muttered, frustrated at not arriving in time. He stood for a moment, panting as he bent to catch his breath. As the adrenaline faded, the cutting chill of the night air replaced it, penetrating his back through the thin cotton shirt.

As he turned back towards his home, he spotted the neighbour from a house three doors down, clutching a small gift bag in one hand, and waving with the other. He realised at once the woman had been seeing off visitors who must have just left and felt foolish. "Good evening, Mrs Macleod," he called, glad she couldn't see the colour of his face. He was also glad he hadn't caught up with the driver of the Lexus. The sight of him holding her visitors over their own car bonnet would not have impressed Elspeth MacLeod.

"Good evening, Grant. I was just waving off my nephew. Hope you and the family are well?"

"Aye, we're all good, thank you. And I hope you are in fine health yourself, Elspeth," he answered as he walked back along the path towards the house and his wife, who would be more than a little confused at his frantic exit.

She was on the doorstep waiting for him.

He heard his neighbours' door click shut.

Jane stood, arms crossed. "Well?" she asked, a mixture of worry and annoyance in her voice. "What was all that about? You damn near gave me a heart attack."

"I'm sorry, love. It was nothing. Just someone visiting the neighbours." He ran a hand over his damp forehead and gave her a sheepish look. "I overreacted. I'm an idiot."

Her expression softened. "That's not like you, love. I've not seen you act like that before. It's this case, isn't it? You've been on edge since it began."

He placed a hand on her shoulder as they went back

inside and closed the door. "Aye, it's getting to me. The people we're looking for... they don't mess around. And sometimes I wonder if they know more about me than I know about them."

Jane pulled him towards the radiator, resting her head on his chest. "You should have put a coat on. You'll catch your death. It's freezing out there."

"I thought I saw a car I recognised." He shrugged. "This case is driving me more than a little crazy. I feel like I'm losing the plot."

She squeezed him. "Grant, I know how seriously you take your cases. You always have. But you need rest like everybody else. You're not a superman, and you can't carry the worry of this investigation home with you every night. You're safe here. We all are. I know it's hard, but try leaving the stress at the door when you leave the office. You'll kill yourself bringing it home."

"You're right." He exhaled, moving the hairs on her head with his breath, still tense with a lingering unease. "I saw a black Lexus and thought..." He trailed off, forcing a smile. "Never mind. You're right. I'm letting it get to me. And it has to stop. I'll drive us all insane. And poor Elspeth Macleod's nephew has no idea how close he came to being ripped from his driver's seat." He laughed, lifting the mood.

She gave his hand a reassuring squeeze. "Come back and sit down. I'll put some rubbish on the TV. Something light-hearted. No crime dramas allowed."

He grinned. "Fair enough. I could use the distraction."

As they settled back into the warm, soft couch, McKenzie glanced once more at the curtains. The shadows outside seemed just a little darker, but he pushed the thought away and focused on Jane nestling in the crook of his arm.

THE FOLLOWING MORNING, the team briefing was about to get underway. McKenzie scribbled on the whiteboard while he waited for everyone to file in. "All right, if I can have all your attention a wee moment?" He turned toward the mostly seated attendees. The briefing was for his team, and members of the uniformed officers helping with searches in Corstophine Woods and around Duddingston Loch. "Thanks for coming. We've got a lot to get through, so we'll need to make a start."

"Helen's just coming," Susan explained.

"Aye, all right. I'll give her another minute or two." He finished writing on the board.

"Sorry, I'm late. Phone call," Helen apologised as she took one of the two chairs still available.

The DI strode to the front. "No worries. I wanted to go over everything we have so far in the investigation into the murders of Caitlin Murray and her friend Ewan MacDonald. I know you've not had it easy over the last couple of weeks. The searches have been extensive and time consuming for our regular officers, I get it, but we have the rocks used as a murder weapon in both cases, and the forensic tests are complete on both. Unfortunately, they got little to nothing from the one fished out of Duddingston Loch. The killer knew what he was doing when he chucked it in the water. But the stone used to kill Caitlin had both her hair and blood on it, and they were able to photograph and lift boot prints left beside it in the mud. There was some evidence the killer tried to smudge these out, but he wasn't completely successful. He would have had limited time to do anything, as the woods were being used by other runners, including Danny Ross, the man who found her. We believe the killer was wearing size ten, Bainsford waterproof walking boots."

He pointed to a photograph of the footwear on the board. "We carried out an initial interview with Danny, but does he own a pair of those boots? If you have a credible suspect who owns a pair of these boots, bring them in for questioning, and send the boots for testing. Unfortunately, the footwear appears to be reasonably new and with no significant wear and tear to distinguish it. However, the killer may not have cleaned the mud off well enough to hide it from forensics. And, if we can find the boots, they could still match them to mud found in the wood or at the lake. Unfortunately, no prints, fibres, or DNA from the killer was left on the rock used to kill Caitlin. This would suggest the killer wore gloves — possibly leather or nitrile gloves — Something that wouldn't leave fibres. If we're lucky, and the gloves were leather, they will have kept them. If so, it's likely there'll be traces of Caitlin's blood, enough to get a match, or traces that would show up with luminol. Questions so far?"

When none was forthcoming, he turned the page in his notebook. "As far as victimology is concerned, we know a great deal more about Caitlin and Ewan, and are developing leads in connection with the businesses both ran, and the estates they left behind. And we are in contact with other divisions in connection with Caitlin and her business dealings abroad. That is still very much a work in progress. But there are other connections we need to know more about, such as the three close friends of the victims. You see, we think the victims knew their killer. These murders were not random acts. Ewan was not a regular visitor to Duddingston. So what took him there that day? And how did the murderer know he would be there? Mr MacDonald did not tell anyone on social media he was going to the Loch, so he had to have told someone in person or via a phone call. Who was that person? I want my team to look closely at the friends of Caitlin and Ewan. Who are they really? What are their histories? And what other connections do they have? Someone they know appears to have taken issue with them all." He turned to underline the names on the board. "Isla Campbell, Douglas MacNeil, and Finlay Scott all received letters threatening their lives. As did Ewan and Caitlin. Why? What angered this person? Was it something they did? Or was it how successful they appeared to others? We know the killer posted the letters in Linlithgow. Unfortunately, we don't have CCTV for the person who posted them. Are any of the five friends connected to someone who lives or has roots in Linlithgow? Go through everything. Who they know, people they've met with whom they may have had issues, and their previous partners. Perhaps someone's ex held a grudge. We believe the letter writer carried out their threats. Why? And why in such a brutal way? It seems to me to be deeply personal, and the answers lie somewhere in the pasts of these five people. We're looking closely at Caitlin Murray. We believe fake passports and regular trips abroad brought her to the attention of security services. Did that result in revenge attacks by a criminal gang? Keep your ears to the ground. Ask your contacts whether there have been any rumours about gang activity or anyone new muscling in on the area."

He walked back towards the seated officers. "Increased, highly visible patrols through major parks are a must from our regular colleagues. The public need to feel safe, and the killer must be made to think twice before attacking in our parks again. These murders were brazen, and I believe it must be someone who lives in our beautiful city. But keep your eyes and ears peeled for anything or anyone out of the ordinary when you are in our green spaces. If my suspicions are wrong, and this is a serial killer attacking at random, he will stake out areas looking for potential victims. So patrols should keep an eye out for the same characters hanging around. And be safe out there."

As they filed out, every one of those present was cognisant of their role, and how important it was to stay vigilant. Some felt more than a little anxious, having family and friends who frequented the parks. Others focused only on what they were going to do to help catch the killer.

13

SKELETONS IN THE CLOSET?

DC Graham Dalgleish removed the scarf from around his neck as he stepped into The Sheep Heid Inn, a historic pub nestled in the heart of Duddingston. The warmth hit him immediately, along with the scent of polished wood, roasted coffee, and the iron-laden tang of warm ale. The low ceiling beams and stone walls gave the place a cosy, timeless feel, while murmured conversations and clinking glasses provided opportunities for frank discussion without being easily overheard.

Graham warmed his hands by the fire crackling in the hearth, after slipping off his overcoat and spotting the man he was meeting, sitting at a corner table near the window.

"Chris," Dalgleish greeted as he approached, placing his coat and scarf over the back of the chair opposite.

Chris Forsyth, a journalist from The Edinburgh Gazette, looked up from his notebook, giving the DC a nod of recognition. A lean man in his late thirties, Forsyth's sharp eyes appeared to miss nothing. He pulled a pen from behind his right ear. "Graham," he said, rising from his seat to shake hands. "Good to see you. You're just in time; I've ordered a pint for me and a coffee for yourself."

"Sounds good," Dalgleish grinned, "Just what I need, it's baltic out there."

"Aye, I ken. So, what brings you to my neck of the woods?" The journalist eyed him, pen lying on his open notebook.

"Thanks for meeting me." Graham leaned forward, elbows on the table. "Listen, we need a favour. We're trying to flush someone out of the shadows, and we think you can help us do it."

Chris's eyes gleamed as he loosened his tie. "Sounds interesting. What's going on?"

Dalgleish lowered his voice. "You'll know we've had two murders recently. Caitlin Murray in Corstorphine Woods and Ewan MacDonald at Duddingston Loch?"

"Aye, it's got everybody frightened around here, I can tell you."

"Well, we have an inkling the killer knew them both, and lay in wait for them where they were murdered."

The journalist narrowed his eyes. "Aye, but Murray ran that route every morning."

"She did, but Ewan did not frequent Duddingston. The two victims knew each other and had received threats previously."

Chris scribbled notes, his pen darting over the page. "That's not public knowledge yet, is it?"

"Not officially. And we would appreciate you not mentioning the letters yet. We'll let you know when you can write about that."

"Got you." Forsyth looked up. "So, we're not looking for someone who is lurking around our parks looking for any available victim?"

"We can't say that for sure. The community should remain vigilant, but we think this killer's vendetta is personal."

"Understood... So where do I come in?"

"We're looking to make a public statement through your newspaper. The killer will scour headlines to see how our investigation is shaping up. We think an article suggesting the killer was someone the victims knew could shake things up a bit, and pressure this killer to double-check stuff; revisit the crime scenes, make a mistake. Someone's hiding something, Chris. And that person had dealings with Caitlin, Ewan, and their friends. We're sure of it."

Forsyth sat back, tapping his pen against the table. "Interesting tactic. You think they'll feel the heat enough to come forward, or inject themselves into your investigation?"

"That's the hope. The idea is to plant the seed that we're closing in. We want them nervous."

Chris pulled at an earlobe. "I can see the angle. But you're asking me to run something speculative, something that might be a stretch for my editor if I can't mention the menacing letters sent to the victims. I'll need to frame it right."

Dalgleish leaned back as his coffee arrived, wrapping his hands around the steaming cup. "I trust you to know what's needed, Chris. We're not looking to accuse anyone outright, only to float the idea that this isn't random. Emphasise the personal connection."

Forsyth glanced out the window at the grey afternoon light filtering through skeletal trees. "I think I can work with that. The Gazette is devouring anything it can get its hands on regarding these murders. It sells a lot of papers and increases our online subscriptions, especially with the local angle. But I'll need a green light from the editor. Though that shouldn't be a problem."

"How soon can you pitch it?" Graham sipped his coffee.

"I'll make the call this afternoon. If he's on board, I may get it done in time for tomorrow's edition. But you'll owe me one. I'll want the scoop on the letters. A photocopy of one of them would be compensation enough."

Dalgleish laughed. "Okay, put it on my tab. But listen... make sure this article hits home. We need the killer to feel like we're breathing down his neck."

Chris nodded. "I'll do what I can."

"Thanks."

They sat in silence for a moment, finishing their coffee and contemplating their next moves. As Dalgleish glanced around the room, he couldn't help but wonder if the killer had ever sat in a place like this, blending into the background; hiding terrible secrets. If their plan worked, the murderer would start feeling hot under the collar. A collar, the DC hoped, that would soon be felt by the hand of the law.

∾

HELEN MCALLISTER HUNCHED over her desk, scrolling through archives as she and Graham researched the backgrounds of Caitlin, Ewan, Isla, Douglas, and Finlay. The two MIT officers had zoned out from the clattering of keys and office chatter behind, their focus wholly on the task at hand.

Dalgleish flipped through pages and pages of search results on the net, with endless clippings and highlighted segments of articles, only some of which were relevant. His brow furrowed in concentration.

McAllister rubbed sore eyes. "Found anything on

Douglas MacNeil yet?" she asked, glancing over. "There's quite a bit on Caitlin and Isla, and a lot of local stuff on Ewan."

Graham shook his head. "Just bits and pieces about him opening his clinic and a few charity events. Nothing that screams skeletons in the closet. And all I've found for Finlay is his mention on the staff list at his school."

"Well, I've just found this..." Helen spun her screen to face him. "It's about his first wife, Miranda. She didn't just leave him while they lived in London, Graham. She disappeared. I mean, proper vanished. It was a full-on missing person's case."

Dalgleish's eyebrows shot up. "Really? She disappeared? How did we not know that?"

"It happened over ten years ago. They were medical students at the time, but it looks like it barely made the news outside of London." McAllister sat back. "All I can find are a few old articles from London newspapers. And that's surprising, because she was a student with everything to look forward to."

"Did they have any thoughts on what might have happened to her?"

"No." She shook her head. "This says someone saw her boarding a train, but no one saw her again after that."

Dalgleish leaned in, scanning the page she had pulled up. "That's definitely something we should look into. Let's get the Met on the phone. Someone over there must remember this case."

∾

A SHORT WHILE LATER, they were on a video call with DCI Adrian Cartwright of the Metropolitan Police, a man with a deep voice and confident air. He appeared on screen to be a well-built man in his early fifties, with thinning hair and a pair of bifocal glasses perched on his nose. In the background lay a desk cluttered with folders, and a whiteboard covered with scribbles.

"Ah, yes, Miranda MacNeil," Cartwright said, chair creaking as he leaned back. "Her case has been gathering dust for nigh-on a decade, but it's technically still open. It was a strange case. One day she was living a normal life, the next, she had vanished without a trace."

"What do you remember of the circumstances?" McAllister asked, notepad at the ready.

Cartwright adjusted his glasses. "Wow, it's been a while... If I remember rightly, her car was found abandoned in the car park of Tring station. That's out in Hertfordshire. Her phone and handbag were still inside, but there was no sign of the woman. We had a single witness who thought they might've seen her board a train heading north, but we could never verify this. CCTV coverage was patchy back then, and we couldn't track her movements beyond the station."

"Were there no other leads?" Dalgleish's brow furrowed.

Cartwright shook his head. "None that held up. We interviewed her young husband, friends, family, and people from her med school, and most said she didn't appear to be unhappy. As far as we could see, there was nothing unusual in the weeks leading up to her disappearance. There was no evidence of foul play, and every sign she may have left under her own steam. Her vehicle was located close to Tring station, fitting with what the only witness had said, about seeing someone who looked like her boarding the train. The problem is, we don't know where she went. It's like she just... vanished."

"What about the witness who said she got on a train? Were they credible?"

"As credible as any. It was an elderly female, if I remember rightly, and we had no reason to doubt her story. She said she couldn't be sure it was Miranda MacNeil, because she didn't know her personally, but she remembered a young woman wearing a navy coat and carrying a tote bag, and said she looked distracted. The coat and bag fitted the description given for what Miranda was wearing when she left the university hospital that day."

Helen exchanged a glance with Graham. "Douglas MacNeil was her husband. What was his story?"

"He appeared, for all intents and purposes, like the grieving husband. Fellow students and professors described him as going round like a lost soul in a daze." Cartwright replied. "And, as far as we could see, he was cooperative, and answered all our questions. Looking back, I'd say he was maybe a little too composed after the first few days. Grief does funny things to people, though, and there was nothing to suggest there had been trouble between them. He'd been seen around the hospital in the hours before his wife's car was abandoned. But between you and me, there was always something off about her car. It was left a couple of streets from the station, which was unusual when there was a perfectly good car park closer by."

"Like the person who left it there had been trying to avoid the station's CCTV?"

"That's what I wondered back then. Of course, Mrs MacNeil may have wanted to avoid being seen, but we scoured all the footage we could, and didn't even find her in the small crowd boarding the train. But then, neither did we see the witness who came forward to say she had seen her. But the witness produced her ticket confirmation, and we also knew the cameras were not recording all the time. We had to accept that we likely didn't have relevant footage."

Dalgleish leaned forward. "And the case went cold…"

"Stone cold," Cartwright confirmed. "Every so often we'd get a tip from someone claiming to have seen her or heard something, but nothing that ever panned out. It's been on the back burner ever since."

Helen jotted all this down. "We'll need access to your files on the case, if that is okay, sir? We're investigating two homicides here in Edinburgh, and both were close friends of Douglas MacNeil."

Cartwright nodded. "I'll have them sent up. I must warn you, there isn't a lot. It's mostly testimony from the witness and friends. Our boss at the time believed the eyewitness and thought Miranda left of her own free will. We were expecting to close the case as soon as she turned up somewhere else. But, as far as we know, she never did. Look, if you uncover anything new, I'd appreciate being kept in the loop. I never liked leaving this one unresolved."

"We'll let you know if we find anything." As the call ended, Dalgleish let out a low whistle. "So, Miranda MacNeil vanished… If Douglas is involved in these murders, his wife's so-called disappearance could have been the blueprint."

McAllister tapped a pen against her notebook, lips pressed together in thought. "And Douglas has been carrying this knowledge around all this time. His wife vanished. And it's not what he told us."

Graham nodded. "Makes you wonder what else he's hiding. Have we found a skeleton in his closet? Or a grave?"

14

THE MISSING SPOUSE

McKenzie was about to enter DCI Sinclair's office when Dalgleish caught up with him.

"Sorry, sir. Are you busy?"

"It can wait..." Grant turned to face him. "What is it?"

"Douglas MacNeil's first wife didn't simply up and leave him. She vanished without a trace?"

"What?"

"It appeared at the time like she took the train to a new identity."

"But your face tells me you don't believe that..." The DI's eyes narrowed.

"They found her car streets away from Tring station, when there was a car park next to it which she could have used."

"Someone wanting to avoid CCTV?"

"That's what we think."

"But Mrs MacNeil may have wanted to get away without being discovered?"

"Perhaps, but how much time would it have bought her? An extra day? Two days? Not enough to make a difference.

What if she never got onto that train? The only witness to her being at the station was a lady who saw someone with a similar coat and bag. She admitted to not being able to recognise Mrs MacNeil, and she hadn't seen a photograph prior to going to the station. She only *thought* she had seen her. That's not confirmation that Miranda MacNeil ever got onto that train."

"You think she was murdered?"

"I'm leaning in that direction. It's been ten years, and no contact with family or friends. And she hasn't used her bank account since. Her coat and phone remained in her vehicle. If she started again, she started with nothing and gave up a very promising medical career. She was a straight-A student. Why would she give that up? And why would she not simply leave her husband? I tell you, Grant, her case sounds fishy as hell to me."

"I agree with you, Graham. But proving it will be difficult after all this time."

"I was hoping you would have a suggestion for where to take it next."

"I think you're right, and Douglas MacNeil needs looking at more deeply, but let's not take our eye off the others. I would suggest having a word with Miranda's family or friends. What did they think about her disappearance, and her marriage to Douglas? If they had concerns, or if there was any evidence of difficulties in the marriage or abuse, we'll have good reason to question him further. What you could also do is have another word with your reporter friend. Maybe he could write a piece on how misfortune has been dogging the friends, mentioning the fact Douglas MacNeil's first wife went missing ten years ago from London. If the doctor is guilty of murder, the extra attention will make him sweat."

"Could work." Graham nodded. "I'll give Forsyth a bell. He might appreciate another prong to this story."

As Dalgleish disappeared down the corridor, the DI checked his watch. Sinclair would have to wait again.

∼

DALGLEISH TOOK a deep breath as he dialled the London number for Mrs Abigail Smallman, Miranda MacNeil's mother. The telephone rang unanswered for a while before she picked up. "Mrs Smallman?" he asked, holding his breath. "I'm Detective Constable Graham Dalgleish, Police Scotland. I wonder if you have time to discuss with me the disappearance of Miranda, your daughter?"

There was an audible gasp on the other end of the line. "Miranda? Have you found her?"

"No, no, I'm sorry, we haven't. But we are re-examining her case, and wondered if you'd be willing to go over the circumstances of her disappearance with us?"

Her sigh conveyed the extent to which his call had got her hopes up. "Of course. I thought for a minute..."

"I know. I'm sorry, there's no news."

"What would you like to know?" Abigail's tired drawl betrayed her weariness at retelling details many times, to no avail. Perhaps this, too, would be a pathway to nothing.

Graham understood, and his heart went out to her. "I believe a witness saw her boarding a train at Tring station in Hertfordshire?"

Mrs Smallman didn't answer right away.

"Was that your understanding?" He was unsure how to read her silence.

"We don't know that for sure," she said, finally. "I had

conflicted feelings about it, I can tell you. Oh, I wanted it to be true. I wanted that more than I can say."

"But you didn't believe it?"

"It made no sense to me... to any of us. Miranda is... or was... so bright. You should have seen her when she was accepted into the medical school in London. She danced round the room like all her Christmases had come at once. It had been her dream since she could remember; our little girl was always patching up her teddies and taking their temperature. To her mind, she'd won the lottery, and she was over the moon. She was only a few months into her course when she began dating Douglas. He was in the same cohort, and their romance was a whirlwind one, for sure. She said he swept her off her feet; couldn't do enough for her. Miranda told me she had never felt so cosseted or received so many compliments from a man."

"I feel a '*but*' coming on?"

Mrs Smallman sighed. "I have to admit to thinking it all seemed a little too good to be true. But I was glad she was happy. Her course was going well, and she achieved high praise for her work. But, after a while, all she ever talked about was Douglas. Myself and her dad worried in case she neglected her studies, but we trusted her to know her own mind. The romance continued, and we could see where it was leading. By early summer, towards the end of her first year, they were already talking about marriage. And, in October of that year, they tied the knot at a local registry office. We had three weeks' notice it was going to happen. Again, my gut told me they were going too fast, but her happiness was important to us, so we went along with it. I live with that every day."

"And how was their marriage, Mrs Smallman?"

"At first, we noticed nothing untoward. The first

Christmas after their wedding, both Miranda and Douglas came to us for dinner on Christmas day. She seemed in her element, but we thought him a little quiet; subdued. She tried getting him up to dance when we put music on after dinner, but he refused. His face was dark, like something had irritated him. He only lightened up at the end, when it was nearly time to go."

"Did Miranda ever discuss him with you?"

"Not with me or her father, no. Apparently, she didn't want to worry us. But she did with her sister, Liz. We didn't find out what she told her until months after she disappeared. Miranda had asked Liz to promise not to say anything to us in case we tried to do something about it."

"What did she tell her sister?"

"She told her that Douglas was moody, and would call her names. She said the name-calling was getting worse, and he was no longer complimentary. Instead, he would criticise all the little things she did or said. And he didn't like her going out with her friends. Oh, he didn't stop her... But he would question her when she got back. Who was she with? Who had she been talking to? Miranda told her sister she found his behaviour suffocating. The following Christmas, when they had been married only fifteen months, he didn't accompany her to see us over Christmas. She came alone. And she wasn't the happy-go-lucky Miranda we had known. I thought she looked pale and thin. And she would zone out. Her eyes would glaze over, and her face looked sad. I assumed she was missing him, but she wouldn't talk about it."

"Did you ever see any bruises on your daughter? Or other marks?" Graham could hear an older male voice in the background.

Mrs Smallman put her hand over the receiver, her voice

Murder in an Edinburgh Park

muffled as she spoke to whoever had joined her. "Sorry, that was Pete, my husband; Miranda's father. You were saying?" she asked.

"I was asking if you suspected Miranda's husband of hurting her? Did you see any marks or bruises on her?"

"No, nothing like that. Although, I guess there could have been in places we couldn't see. But we didn't notice any, and she never mentioned violence."

"What was she like in the weeks prior to her disappearance?"

Abigail was silent for a couple of seconds before answering. "She went missing the summer after she came to us alone for Christmas. They said she boarded a train at Tring station, and they found her belongings in her car, parked streets away. And I'll tell you now, we didn't understand it. We couldn't accept that she would just go away like that without talking to us first. Or, at least, without discussing it with her sister. It made no sense. As far as the university was concerned, she was on course to get a first-class medical degree. Her work standard had slipped a little, but not enough to cause them concern. So we couldn't understand why she would leave, unless it was that she was unhappy in her marriage. But then, why hadn't she spoken to one of us?"

"How did Douglas react at the time?"

"Well, that's what confused us... We couldn't have faulted him at all. He looked distraught, as you would expect, and called us every few days to ask if we had heard anything. He talked to police, and they said he appeared to have told them everything he knew. And, like I said, someone saw Miranda boarding a train. We knew she had been unhappy. We thought maybe she just needed to get away for a while; to be by herself. But then, as the months rolled on, we felt it wasn't right; that something was wrong. That's when we really questioned things. By then, however, the Met police had rolled back their appeals for information, believing she had left of her own accord. They told us she was a free citizen and had every right to disappear, if that is what she wanted to do. We felt helpless. We put up posters. Myself, her dad, and Liz pounded the streets for weeks, but we never had a decent lead. We investigated alleged sightings only to discover they were of other people. None of them led to her whereabouts. And then, a year later, we learned Douglas MacNeil was dating again. Six months more, and he had moved the new woman in. That hurt, I can tell you. It was like he rubbed Miranda out, erasing her as though she had never existed. It was at that point I felt total despair. The rest of the world had moved on, but we couldn't. I still look for her all the time, when I am in crowds, or standing at a station. And just now, when you called, my heart lurched."

"I know, I'm so sorry." Dalgleish felt her pain. "Do you know anything about MacNeil's current relationship?"

"No, we don't hear from him. In fact, I don't think he has ever reached out to us since he began dating the new woman. I tried calling him several years back, to see if he had heard anything from Miranda, but he'd changed his number. I couldn't reach him. So I'm afraid I can't comment on his current relationship. You would have to speak to the lady directly."

"We may just do that, Mrs Smallman," Graham advised. "But thank you for talking with me today. Your information has been very useful, and I can promise you we will chase all of this up. I can't promise we'll be able to find your daughter, but we will scrutinise everything we can during our investigation."

"Will you let me know?" She sounded afraid of hoping too much.

"We will tell you the results of our enquiry, yes."

"Thank you," she said.

"I'll be in touch." As he put the phone down, Graham had a nagging feeling in the pit of his stomach. Something had happened to Miranda Smallman, and that something was bad. He would put money on the fact she never boarded that train. Perhaps she had been right to fear her husband. But if her skeleton was hiding in Douglas MacNeil's closet, the DC was determined that Edinburgh MIT would find it so Miranda could finally rest in peace.

～

"Did you get anything?" McKenzie asked, as he approached the Dalgleish's desk.

"Aye, I'd say so. Douglas MacNeil was controlling with his wife, and Miranda's mum reckons her daughter was afraid of him."

"Really?" The DI mulled this over. "Make sure you speak to Chris Forsyth," he said. "Ask him to run that piece on Miranda MacNeil. Let's see if we can bring pressure to bear on the doctor. If he is guilty of harming his wife, it should rattle him."

15

CONFRONTATION

Dalgleish leaned against the iron railings overlooking Princes Street Gardens, the faint hum of Edinburgh's evening rush hour behind him. He'd been waiting only a few minutes when Chris Forsyth appeared, a black leather satchel slung over his shoulder; phone in hand. The journalist cut a solid figure as he approached; eyes darting around like he was continuously looking for a story.

"You're here already... I like that." Forsyth slipped his phone into his coat pocket. "I'm surprised you wanted to see me again so soon. Is something up? You sounded cryptic on the phone."

Graham gestured towards a nearby bench. "This shouldn't take long, but we need your help again."

Forsyth's eyebrows rose, but he sat as directed. "I assume it's related to your investigation? Don't worry, I can be discreet when I need to."

"That's what we're banking on..." Dalgleish lowered his voice as they sat. "You already know we're looking into the murder of Caitlin Murray and Ewan MacDonald..."

"Uh huh, sure." Forsyth nodded.

"Well, there's a potential link to a cold case involving their friend Douglas MacNeil. His first wife, Miranda, disappeared ten years ago, and there's every reason to suspect she didn't leave of her own accord."

Forsyth whistled. "You think MacNeil killed her?"

Graham flicked a glance around. There was no-one nearby as dusk closed in, only a developing mist which deepened with the fading light. "We can't say that. We don't know. But the circumstances are suspicious, and we're not ruling it out." Dalgleish folded his arms, his gaze fixed on the mist. He lifted his collar as the penetrating chill got to his neck. "The thing is, we need to turn up the heat on Dr MacNeil. Our DI suggests we use your skills to... stir the pot. Get him hot under the collar, so to speak."

The journalist's eyes shone. "You want me to write something about Miranda? Speculative? Or factual?"

"Factual," Graham directed. "But framed in a way that gets his attention. Maybe a piece on the group of friends, and how tragedy seems to follow them around. Caitlin's murder, Ewan's murder, and Miranda MacNeil's mysterious disappearance, all tragic events. We need enough in the article to make him squirm, if he was involved, without crossing the line into libel."

The journalist regarded him for a moment, arms resting on the backrest of the bench. "I see what you're trying to do, but do you really think this'll rattle him?"

"It will if he had a hand in any of those events. The pressure of public scrutiny could make him slip up. He's a cool customer. And whoever killed Caitlin and Ewan is careful, and forensically aware. If our killer is MacNeil, I don't see him making mistakes otherwise. We are talking about an intelligent man. A general practitioner. He's going to be careful."

"And if he's innocent?"

"Then he'll simply appreciate you raising the profile of his missing wife. If he is innocent, he will have spent a long time wondering about her. Finding his wife would bring him closure, at least. And he would want Caitlin's and Ewan's murderer caught, if he was not involved."

"But there's a risk, isn't there?" Forsyth pressed. "If he was involved, this could spook him into silence. Or worse, push him to cover his tracks even more thoroughly."

Dalgleish nodded. "That is a potential downside, I admit. But it's a calculated risk we're taking. Our DI believes the risk will be worthwhile. If we can provoke a reaction, it could give us the break we need."

Forsyth tilted his head, studying the DC. "And you? What do you think?"

Dalgleish hesitated. "I agree it has its risks, but it's also the best shot we have of causing him to slip up. MacNeil's clever. He knows how to keep himself in the clear. But public exposure might crack that composure."

The reporter tapped his fingers on the backrest. "I think I can work with this. I'll draft something to highlight the tragic pattern, but stop short of pointing of fingers. But if this blows up, you're shielding me, yeah? I don't want to find myself in a headlock with a killer."

"You have my word," Graham assured him. "We'll protect you."

The journalist stood, brushing off his coat. "Alright, Graham... I'll do the piece. I'll need your contacts for the missing person case, and permission to call them. And I'll send you the draft before it goes live, so you can give it the nod. Sound fair?"

"Very." Dalgleish rose to his feet. "Thanks, Chris. Let's hope it shakes something loose."

Forsyth gave a mock salute. "I hope your DI knows what he's doing."

"So do I." Graham grinned. "Thanks for the help."

"No worries." As Forsyth disappeared towards the gates, Dalgleish lingered by the bench, casting his eyes around a park shrouded in mist. Was their killer lurking in the shadows? He paid extra attention to those shadows as he made his way back to his vehicle.

∼

Isla stared at the screen, hands shaking as she scrolled back to the photograph accompanying Chris Forsyth's article about Douglas's missing wife in the Gazette. She was sure it was the same oak tree, its distinct silhouette unmistakable as it appeared in the backdrop of one of Forsyth's images of Tring Station. She held her breath, holding up Caitlin's photograph for comparison. If it was indeed the same tree, why had her friend asked her to look after the image? Had she been afraid of something? Or someone?

Isla's heart thumped as pieces of the puzzle slotted together in her head, forming a picture so chilling she had to steady herself against the edge of the desk. Miranda MacNeil, the missing wife of their friend, Douglas. Caitlin had never discussed it with her, even though she had known him through this dark period in his life. The two of them had carried on communicating, even while studying hundreds of miles from one another. MacNeil had always said Miranda left him for another man. Had Caitlin suspected something else? Or did she know something? Was she given the photograph by MacNeil? Or did she take it from him without his knowledge? Had he killed his wife so he could start dating another woman?

The more Isla Campbell thought about it, the more she felt Caitlin must have suspected MacNeil capable of murder. Why else would she have given her best friend that photograph for her to look after it? It wasn't merely a keepsake. This was potential evidence.

The designer's thoughts whirled. Caitlin wouldn't have kept the photograph without a reason. Did she confront him? Is that why she ended up bludgeoned atop Corstophine Hill? And if Miranda never left to be with another man, as MacNeil claimed, then where was she?

Her gaze flicked back to the oak tree. The realisation dawning like a thunderclap. Caitlin may have suspected MacNeil of burying his wife under that tree.

A wave of nausea rolled over her. Clutching her phone, she pulled up the article again, rereading the lines about Miranda's disappearance, her vehicle abandoned at Tring Station. Isla had never had cause to question MacNeil's story, but now the lies seemed glaring. And Caitlin had known both Miranda and Douglas. What else had she known?

The designer felt she had to act, but do what? Call McKenzie? Tell him about the photograph? She had no proof of its significance, only that it was almost certainly a tree near Tring station. But that wasn't proof of very much. No, she needed more before going to McKenzie. And there was only one way to get it.

∼

Isla Campbell pushed open the door to the surgery with a

clang and strode to the front desk. "I need to see Dr MacNeil urgently. Is he in?"

The salt-and-pepper-haired woman behind the desk regarded the designer through her bifocals, a stern look on her face. "I'm sorry, if it's an emergency appointment you're wanting, you'd best let us know the problem and, if we agree it is an emergency appointment you're needing, we'll assign you the next available doctor. But you should ring us up to make an emergency appointment, not coming in here demanding to be seen."

Isla inhaled, puffing out her chest. "You listen here... Tell Douglas MacNeil that Isla Campbell is here to see him, and it would be in his best interests to speak with me at his earliest convenience!" She turned on her heel after the last, swinging her bag for effect as she strode to a seat in the corner, away from other people in the waiting room.

The receptionist's mouth became a thin line as she stood abruptly, chair squeaking in protest. "Wait here," she said, without looking at Isla, and disappeared through a door behind the desk.

Isla perched on the edge of the plastic chair, arms crossed tightly. Inquisitive stares from the other attendees did little to soften the knotted tension in her chest. Nor did the muttered conversations between them, accompanied by sniggers. But this was too important to put off. She checked her watch, nagging questions in her mind drowning out the coughs, shuffling of magazines, and a child's restless crying. She felt distant from it all, her thoughts locked firmly on the man she had thought a friend, and the web of lies she now believed surrounded him.

Media savvy, the designer recognised a police pressure tactic when she saw one. There was a reason the Gazette had printed that story. The thought gnawed at her, twisting and turning as it morphed through murky possibilities. And who was the most likely person to know where Ewan would be that day besides Caitlin, if she had still been alive? Douglas. They normally played squash on that day. It all made sense.

The receptionist reappeared a moment later, her expression more acerbic than before. "Dr MacNeil will see you now. Room three, down the corridor and to the left."

"Thank you," Isla said curtly, rising to her feet.

The walk down the narrow corridor filled her with doubt. What if she had it wrong and her suspicions were misplaced? She risked losing a valued friendship. But anger at his lies spurred her on, heels tapping on linoleum tiles, marking time until she reached room three.

She hesitated, hand hovering over the door handle. What if she was wrong? She could still turn back.

But then she remembered the worried look on Caitlin's face when she'd mentioned needing to talk to Douglas. There had been something in that faraway gaze. Isla hadn't paid it much attention at the time, but the article had brought it back with a sharp focus. And Ewan... Who else would have known Ewan would go to Duddingston Loch that day? And how did they know? Douglas MacNeil had some answering to do.

Heart thudding, she pushed open his door.

Douglas sat at the desk, white coat spotless; stethoscope coiled like a snake about his neck. His expression was one of careful neutrality, but the designer noticed the way his knuckles whitened around the pen he was holding.

"Isla," he greeted, his tone light, but without a smile. "This is unexpected. How can I help?" He swung his chair around to face her.

She shut the door, leaning back against it. "I'd like to

know why you lied to us, Douglas," she said, words stiff from a mouth suddenly dry. "Your wife didn't leave you for another man, did she? She vanished without a trace. Not even her family has ever heard from her since. She left everything behind, including a promising future as a doctor. Why would she do that? And why would you lie about it to your best friends?"

MacNeil's brow furrowed as he parsed what she had said. "Look, I don't know what you've been reading, but my wife-"

"How did you know I had read something, Douglas?" Isla cut him off, her voice trembling. "Was it because you also read this?" She took out a folded, crumpled page torn from that morning's Gazette and held it up for him to see. "This journalist seems to think bad luck has followed our little group around. And he's right, isn't he? It has. Only I don't believe in bad luck like that."

"I don't know what you're-"

"I know about Miranda, about how she disappeared from Tring station. And I know Caitlin went to see you in the days before she died. She wanted to talk to you about something, didn't she? What was it? Did she know about Miranda?"

He stood, his movement slow, calculated. "Caitlin was a good friend," he said, his voice softer, almost mournful. "If she'd had something to say, I would have listened. We'd known each other all our lives, virtually. There wasn't much she didn't know about me."

"Did she know about your wife?"

"She had always known. That's why what you're saying makes no sense. Why would Caitlin suddenly want to talk to me about my lost wife after all these years? Listen to yourself. You're making no sense, Isla."

"Except, she gave me this, and asked me to look after it." Isla held up the dog-eared photo of a hill with a lone oak tree standing proudly atop it. "She didn't tell me where this was taken, or why she had it. She only told me to keep it safe in my purse. I asked her why, but she wouldn't say. She told me she would come to me when she needed it back. It seemed important to her."

"What's your point, Isla?"

"Tring station is the place your wife allegedly disappeared from. They found her car abandoned not far away, didn't they? I know this because I read it in here?" She tapped the article. "Did you take this photograph, Douglas?"

"You're acting crazy."

"Were you looking for this photo when you went to Caitlin's flat after she was murdered?"

"What?" He screwed his face up.

"I know you went there. The police officers asked me if I knew anyone who wore Ralph Loren, Polo Red. I've never asked you what you wear whenever we go to dinner, but I went to the chemist and asked to smell a tester. And you wear Polo Red. Someone had been in Caitlin's flat after her murder wearing that aftershave."

"You're acting crazy, Isla." His voice was calm, but the muscles in his face tightened.

"Then why did she give me this picture? I didn't put two and two together until I saw this article. But I know she wanted to talk to you days before she was murdered," Isla pressed, stepping closer. "Why was she worried? What was it she needed to talk to you about? Was it your wife? Where did she get this picture?"

MacNeil's cheeks reddened, and for a moment, Isla thought he might lose his composure. But he sighed, shaking his head. "Look, you've got this all wrong." He ran a hand through his hair. "I didn't hurt Miranda. And as for Caitlin… there's more to that story than you think."

"So tell me," Isla demanded.

He studied her, his gaze piercing. "Fine," he said at last. "I'll tell you everything. But not here. This isn't the place for it. Time is moving on, and I still have patients waiting to see me."

Isla hesitated. She no longer trusted him, but her need for answers outweighed her fear. "Where, then? It has to be a public place."

"Very well. There's a decent cafe on Home Street. It's quiet; we can talk there. He checked his watch. Can you make it for three-thirty?" He stepped closer, his voice low. "I have no reason to lie to you, Isla. But you need to hear the truth from me, not from some journalist with an agenda."

Isla turned her gaze to the frosted window of his office, brow furrowed as she weighed the pros and cons. Finally, she nodded, her words clipped. "Three-thirty. Don't be late."

She left without another word, but her heart pounded painfully as she walked away. The air in the corridor felt heavy, oppressive, as though warning her to change her mind. Cancel the meeting. Caitlin's knowledge may have been the reason she lost her life. If the designer wasn't careful, she could be next. But Isla couldn't stop. Not now. Not until she knew the truth. She took comfort in knowing the encounter would be in a well-lit, public venue, not the lonely dark wood where her best friend had met her brutal end.

16

A RISK TOO FAR?

The Books N' Cup Cafe on Home Street, near The Meadows, a large public park in the city's south, was far from full as Isla pushed open the door and strode in. She shook her umbrella outside of the entrance to free it from the feather-like snow, which began falling only minutes before.

Stone walls, wood flooring, rustic rope chandeliers, and leather seating gave the place a luxurious, old-world charm. Books shelved in alcoves, the smell of coffee, and the aroma of home-cooked pastries helped calm her nerves, at least until the man she suspected of having all the answers arrived. She ordered an oatmeal, flat white, while she waited.

He brushed snow from his hair as he walked through the door, removing his overcoat.

Isla swallowed, hand shaking as she placed her coffee cup back on its saucer.

He ordered a macchiato at the counter before walking to her table. "I didn't mean to keep you waiting," he said, placing his overcoat over the back of the chair opposite. His voice was gentle, but he didn't take his eyes off her face, and there was a darkness to his.

"I wondered whether you had changed your mind," she said, voice rattling. She cleared her throat.

He loosened his tie, undoing the top button of his white cotton shirt. "I don't know what you think you know," he said, voice low like a growl, "but you are way off piste. And how dare you come crashing into my surgery like that, Isla, demanding to see me..." He flicked a glance around the coffee shop, making sure they were not being watched. "What will people think?"

"Did Caitlin know all along?" The designer's eyes bored into him as though reading his soul.

"Know what all along?"

"That you killed your wife."

"Don't be ridiculous," he hissed. "Listen to yourself. You're supposed to be my friend, but you read a piece in the paper about my wife vanishing when we were both medical students and, in your eyes, I must be guilty of her murder. How does that equate? Caitlin's and Ewan's deaths have made you unhinged. You can't draw conclusions from a newspaper article, especially one which, in itself, doesn't accuse me of anything." He softened his tone once more. "Look, I know the last few weeks have been hard... Hellish, even. But seeing murderers around every corner will not help you, myself, or Finlay. We are frightened too, you know?"

"But there's this, isn't there," Isla returned, taking the dog-eared photo from her purse and laying it on the table in front of him. "Look at it, Douglas. Is that where you buried Miranda?"

He leaned in, his face like thunder. "Look, I don't know

what you think you see here, but you didn't know the first thing about Caitlin, or why she gave you that photograph."

"What do you mean, I didn't know her? We were best friends." Isla's face furrowed. "We told each other everything."

"But I bet she didn't go into specifics about this photo, did she?"

The designer swallowed.

"No, I didn't think so. She gave it to you, but didn't tell you why. Maybe this was insurance." He picked up the photograph. "You can't say this is near Tring station. It's a tree. It could be anywhere."

"Why else would she have given it to me in the way she did? It was important. Significant."

"Look, there are things you don't... Oh, Jesus... I don't know if I should even say this."

"Say what?"

He leaned back in his chair. "If I tell you, I... Look, it doesn't matter. Forget it."

"What?" Her eyebrows knitted in frustration. "You can't begin a story and not finish it. We're not children. I can cope with whatever you have to say, Douglas."

He sighed. "Very well... Did you ever wonder what Caitlin did on those frequent trips away? Um? Did you ask her what she did?"

"What do you mean? She was buying coffee; meeting new people; finding plantations and small businesses to work with."

"Oh, sure... She was doing all of that, of course, but what else?"

Isla's brow furrowed. "There wasn't anything else... Was there?"

"You never suspected her of hiding something?"

"Spit it out, for God's sake. What else was she doing?"

He leaned in close again. "She was-"

The young woman from the counter placed his macchiato on the table next to him. "You forgot to wait for this," she said.

"Oh, so I did." He took a deep breath, barely looking at the girl who had come from behind her counter to deliver his drink. He didn't thank her, but returned his attention to Isla. "Your friend, our friend," he corrected, "Caitlin was secretly working for the intelligence services."

"What?" Isla snorted. "You expect me to believe that?"

"It's true." He sat back, self-satisfied. "You recall the outfits in her wardrobe?"

"Yes..."

"And the wigs?"

"She didn't wear them that often."

"Didn't she?"

"Well, maybe on the odd evening out, if it was a themed night or something."

"Then why have them? And she must have had at least eight or nine. Didn't you ask her what she wanted them for?"

"We used to parade about in them for a giggle. Wigs are not unusual in my line of work, you know." Isla pouted. "A woman can change her look if she feels like it. It's called self-expression."

"But she wasn't in your line of work, was she? Caitlin ran a coffee business, didn't she?"

Isla didn't answer, her mind mulling over his words.

"And what about the passports?"

"Passports?"

"You never needed to borrow a tampon from her?"

"What?"

"That's where she kept them... in an old tampon box." He snorted.

"I always carry my own." She frowned.

"Yes, well, she had five or six fake passports, all of them stamped with countries in Asia, South America, and the like. You mean to tell me you never saw them? It made the wigs make sense, I can tell you."

"How come you knew about them?"

"I've known what Caitlin was up to for many years. We've known each other since learning to walk. There wasn't much I didn't know about her."

"So, what are you trying to tell me?"

"I'm saying there was a lot more to her work trips than met the eye, and she met with dangerous people on some of those trips. She told me a long time ago that if anything happened to her, I was to explain to her parents what she did and why she did it. And then ask them never to tell."

"And did you?"

"Not yet."

"I don't believe you." Isla folded her arms. "I'd have known."

"She went undercover on several occasions. You must remember when she came back looking like death warmed up? Gaunt, dark under the eyes; needed feeding up? You remember her like that, don't you?"

"Well, yes, but-"

"Did you never ask yourself why she was in that state? How did sauntering around the globe looking for fair trade coffee leave her in such a mess? Why on earth did she come back in that condition? Come on, Isla, think about it."

"She'd have told me if she was doing anything dangerous." Confusion contorted the designer's face. Had Caitlin been leading a double life and hiding it from her?

"She wasn't supposed to tell anyone. If I hadn't known her all her life, she likely would not even have told me. And it wasn't as though she just came out and said it. I badgered her for ages because I knew that woman like the back of my hand. I knew something was up with those trips. Sometimes, when she came back, she looked like she'd seen a ghost... Or had a very close shave. These were deadly gangs she went after. They'd have killed her as look at her if they'd known who she really was. And," his face softened, the angry look replaced by one of resignation, "sadly, I think at some point they must have found out."

Isla leaned back in her chair, her eyes clouded. Of course, it all made a sort of sense. There had been many odd things over the years. And, if the designer hadn't been so busy going here and there herself, she would likely have given Caitlin an inquisition just like Douglas had. He was right about the wigs, and the state she sometimes returned in. Their friend had lost nearly two stone on one occasion. There had been hardly anything left of her. It had given Isla a hell of a shock. Caitlin explained it away, saying she had been too excited to eat after discovering this or that bean, and these or those lovely people. Perhaps, after all, there had been much more to it. "And the photo?" She referred to the image now on the table in front of him. "That tree?"

He shrugged. "I guess it was significant to her for a reason... But she never went into detail about her intelligence operations. That was something she never did. I knew there had been missions. I recognised the signs. But she never talked about them with me, only that one time, when she swore me to secrecy."

Isla still wasn't sure. "When did she tell you about it?" Her eyes scoured his face.

"Years ago, when she asked me to speak to her parents if

anything happened to her." He paused. "Come to think of it, she may have mentioned it again after we received those death threats." He sighed. "She was worried she had somehow put us in danger."

"Why didn't you say something?"

"I couldn't, I'd promised."

"Have you spoken to police? Told them about her work for intelligence agencies?"

"No, like I said, I promised not to talk unless it was to her parents... which I have not yet had the courage to do."

"Well, you must go to the police with what you know."

"Will you help me?" he asked, in a childlike manner which threw her.

"Help you, how?"

"Come with me, or at least help me work out how to put it to them."

"Why don't you just tell them?"

"How do I do that without compromising whatever mission she was involved with?"

Isla scratched her head. "I don't know-"

"Walk with me," he said, his hand hovering over hers before withdrawing, as if sensing her unease. "Let's finish this coffee and take a walk through The Meadows. It'll help us think."

Isla hesitated, her grip tightening on the photograph. She couldn't shake the memory of Caitlin's gaunt face after her last trip abroad, nor the urgency with which she had handed over the picture. It all seemed to fit now, yet still felt impossibly surreal.

"Fine," she said, her voice stiff. "I'll walk. But this doesn't mean I trust you, Douglas. And when we're done, you must tell DI McKenzie everything."

"Uderstood, Isla." He nodded, draping his coat over his arm. "Shall we?"

∽

"Do you think we've given him enough time?" Susan Robertson plopped a coffee in front of the DI as he finished catching up with emails.

"Who, MacNeil?"

"Aye, paper's been out a day and a half. Even if he hasn't seen Forsyth's article himself, someone is bound to have mentioned it to him in the surgery."

"That's what I'm hoping." McKenzie checked his watch. "Yes, I think we'll give him a ring; see how he reacts."

"I've got his details here." She held up her notebook.

"I'll call his mobile first." McKenzie grabbed his phone. "If he's busy, I'll leave a message asking him to call us."

The doctor's phone rang several times before someone switched it off.

McKenzie frowned, clicking off the call and staring at his mobile in thought.

"Not answering? I thought you were going to leave a voicemail."

Grant shook his head, dialling again. "Didn't get the chance. I think he stopped the call. I'm giving it another go."

"No luck?" Susan asked, on seeing him frown again.

"He must be with a patient. I think he's stopping the calls. And I canna leave him a voicemail."

"Maybe ring the surgery. Leave a message with his receptionist. He won't want to mess with her. She'll have him calling us as soon as he's free."

McKenzie got the number from Susan's pad and dialled.

"Aye, good afternoon. Can I speak to Dr MacNeil, please? It's DI Grant McKenzie."

"Oh, I'm sorry..." The receptionist hesitated. "He's not here. He left not half an hour ago."

"Did he say where he was going?"

"No, I'm afraid he didn't. He cancelled his last few patients and said something had come up."

"Did he tell you what the problem was?"

"No, but it was right after a wee crabbit woman came in demanding to see him. She had a face like thunder."

"His partner?"

"No, I'd never seen her before."

"What was her name?"

"Och, I don't know if I should say... Patient confidentiality..."

"We're police officers."

"Hang on a moment. I'll just check the book."

McKenzie shot a look at Robertson, shrugging his shoulders.

"Right, here it is. She gave her name as Isla Campbell."

"Isla?" The DI checked his watch. "And what time did the doctor leave?"

"It would have been just after three."

"Thanks. Look if he comes back? Ask him to ring me. Tell him it's urgent."

"All right, Inspector, I'll tell him."

Grant turned to Susan. "He went out. Left in a hurry after Isla Campbell went to see him. Told the secretary to cancel the rest of his appointments."

"Oh, crap. We'd better call her."

"Aye, let's get her details up and try her landline and mobile."

Dalgleish and McAllister joined them as the DI

punched Isla's number into his phone. There was no answer on her landline.

"Try her mobile." Susan underlined the number on her pad.

"It's ringing," he said, putting a finger in the opposite ear to better hear. "Hello, Ms Campbell?"

"DI McK-" she began before the call cut off.

"Isla? Isla?" He dialled the number again. This time, there was no answer. Grant turned to the others. "She got cut off. Sounded like she was out in the open somewhere."

"Where?" Susan frowned.

"I don't know, but I've got a bad feeling..." McKenzie stood to rattle off instructions. "Graham, track her phone signal; get tech on it now. Helen, check with her colleagues and friends. Find out if anyone knows where she is."

Susan interjected, "What about MacNeil? If she was with him—"

"Aye, that's what I'm afraid of. Let's get his vehicle flagged and an alert out. He's not at the surgery, but he can't have gone far." McKenzie grabbed his coat, already striding for the door. "We'll split up. If Isla's in trouble, we need to move fast."

"Should we call in uniformed officers to assist?" Dalgleish asked, dialling their tech team.

"Aye, we best alert them. Susan and I will head out that way." McKenzie scanned the growing darkness outside. "If she went to meet him, it's possible they're somewhere close to his surgery. Where's the nearest park from there?"

"That would be The Meadows, sir."

"Right, so it would. Susan? You happy to come?"

"I am. Let me grab my coat."

Snow was falling heavy as Grant and Susan headed to their vehicle. A veil of white was already settling over the city. As McKenzie stepped into the cold, his phone buzzed. It was Graham, with news from the tech team.

"Sir, we've got Isla Campbell's phone location. It's showing movement near The Meadows."

His brow furrowed. "Request uniformed officers go to the location with dogs, and armed backup if there's a unit free. We're on our way." He motioned for Dalgleish to follow as they rushed to the car. "If MacNeil's with her, she could be in danger."

17

A MENACING EVIL

"I know what you're up to on these mysterious trips of yours." MacNeil grinned, his voice light, but his eyes had narrowed. "You might fool the others, but I can tell when you're on your little top-secret missions." He crouched, shielding his eyes dramatically as though scanning the trees for enemies. Standing, he brushed invisible dust from his knees. "Don't worry, Caitlin, darling, I won't say a word."

"You'd better not," she replied, forcing a smile as she reached out to shove his shoulder. "One phone call from me..." Her voice trailed off, but the weight of her words lingered between them.

MacNeil's face hardened instantly. The smile lines vanished, his mocking demeanour replaced by something colder, harder. "You wouldn't dare."

"Neither would you." She kept her voice steady, but her stomach churned. Fraught nerves buzzed, her earlier bravado ebbing away. She thought she knew how to handle him—calm, playful, never pushing too far—but she'd seen the cracks before, those fleeting moments when the mask slipped. She didn't like what she glimpsed underneath.

His face creased, and for a moment, he looked almost vulnerable. "Seriously, I didn't mean to kill her. It wasn't supposed to happen. It was a... momentary loss of control." His voice cracked as he pleaded. "I've regretted it every single day. You know that. You must have seen how tortured I was. I didn't sleep for weeks. Some nights, I still don't."

Caitlin swallowed, her throat dry. Did he expect her pity? She kept her expression neutral, but blood thundered in her ears. "Then why not come clean?"

"I can't." He shook his head, gazing away. "You wouldn't understand."

"It would stop those sleepless nights." The words came out quieter than she intended, barely a whisper. Caitlin tried not to blink as his eyes flicked back to her face, defiant and unyielding. She kept control. She couldn't let him see her fear.

"Would it?" His voice echoed her softness, but with an edge. "Would you also come clean?"

"With what?" Her frown deepened, chest tight. Where was he going with this?

"With all the things you've been hiding from your family; your closest friends."

"That's not the same," she shot back, tension in her rising voice. "I have done nothing illegal, Douglas. The secrets I keep are for our country. There's no comparison." She regretted the words as soon as they left her mouth. She had revealed too much all those years ago. Given him bullets to use against her. She had to bring him back onside.

He laughed, a bitter cackle, turning his back to her. "So, what are you saying? That I should confess now? After ten years? Throw my whole life away? Everything I have achieved? My practice? You know they wouldn't understand. I'd spend the best part of my life in prison. Out here, I am helping sick people get well, leading an honourable life, living with someone else."

"I'm saying you should do the right thing." She kept her voice *calm. "I believe you when you say you didn't mean to hurt Miranda. But do you think she sleeps soundly while her remains lie buried in unconsecrated ground?"*

He stood still for a moment, shoulders rising and falling with slow, measured breaths. He turned back to her, a lopsided smile creeping across his face. "Maybe you're right. Maybe I should think about it."

"Do you mean that?" She straightened, relieved his temper had turned a corner.

"Of course." His smile widened, but didn't quite reach his eyes. "Why wouldn't I?"

∼

Isla's phone trilled from her bag. "Hang on." She reached inside for it. "Ach, it's DI McKenzie. What does he want now?" She spoke into the phone. "DI McK-"

MacNeil snatched it from her hand, switching it off before she could argue with him.

"What the hell? What are you doing? Give me ma bloody phone back, Douglas." Her eyes shot fire at him, her accent deepening as the adrenaline rose. "I dunna ken what he wants. It could be something urgent."

"We have important things to discuss, Isla, and we don't need his interruptions. You and I can speak to the DI together later, after we've talked."

She regarded him warily, snow falling thick from a rapidly darkening sky. "I think we should go back to the cafe," she said, hearing the tremble in her own voice.

"But it's not private in there, Isla." He pocketed her phone.

She swallowed, throat becoming dry. "It's getting dark."

"It won't take long."

A female approached, walking her dog.

Isla stepped forward, about to say something.

MacNeil grabbed her arm. "Don't," he muttered, steering her away from the woman with the pooch. "You wanted me to tell you about Caitlin's work. Well, I'll talk if you'll listen"

Isla turned to him. "Give me my phone, Douglas. This has gone far enough. You don't need me to tell you what to say to the DI. You know a lot more than I do. So why are we here?" The tremor in her voice was all too audible.

"Keep it down," he ordered. "I'm only worried we could compromise the important work she did; taint her legacy. Those gangs don't mess about Isla."

"I don't believe you." She took a step back. "I'm leaving, Douglas. If you don't give me back my phone, I'll report it stolen by you."

"Very well." He sighed, reaching into his pocket and pulling it out. "Here…"

As she stepped forward to take it, he made to grab her, catching her coat.

She freed herself from the garment and set off running back the way they had come. Snow had already obscured the path, and she stumbled as her feet hit soft ground. He was so close behind.

18

FIGHT AT THE MEADOWS

Duddingston Loch lay serene in the winter sunshine, its glassy surface disturbed only by the faint ripples of a moorhen paddling near the reeds. The last of the morning's mist curled around the banks, clinging to skeletons of frosted brambles. Ewan breathed deep, filling his lungs with air that stung, and lifted his eyes to a sky broken only by the occasional lonely cloud.

From his canvas messenger bag, he pulled six red roses, their soft petals tinged with brown from being out of water for so long; their sweet perfume fading, but still there. He brought them to his nose, inhaling. "These are for you, dearest Caitlin," he said aloud, voice cutting through the stillness. The first rose flew out onto the water, its crimson head bobbing gently on the loch's surface.

His mind slipped back to a bright summer day years before, when he and Caitlin had cycled to the village, stopping at the kirk and laughing over a makeshift picnic by the loch. The sunlight had rendered everything golden, glinting off Caitlin's hair as she leaned her bike against the garden wall. She had been radiant that day, her excitement about starting her business infectious, her laughter rippling like the water. He had been too shy to tell *her how beautiful she looked then, too caught up in that moment's buzz.*

He blinked away the memory, his gaze falling to the bench they'd sat on. It still stood, empty and weathered, near the water's edge. He sighed, murmuring, "I hope you're smiling up there, Caitlin," and lifted his eyes to the heavens.

One by one, he tossed the remaining roses into the loch. Each dipped, then rose again, spreading in a slow arc across the water like large drops of blood. "Rest in peace, my dear friend," he whispered, his voice lost to the chatter of birds and the stirring of reeds in the breeze.

He stood, closing the bag, fingers trembling with the cold—or perhaps something else. He didn't hear the careful footsteps behind, muffled by damp ground. Nor did he notice the figure shadowing his every movement, waiting for the right moment to pounce.

A whisper of air was his only warning before the first blow landed. Pain exploded across the back of his skull, a white-hot flash that blurred his vision and sent his knees buckling. The loch wavered before him like a mirage as he stumbled, gasping, hand outstretched to steady himself. He tried turning, but the second blow descended with a sickening thud.

The world turned dark before he hit the ground.

∽

ISLA STUMBLED, falling headlong into snow-covered grass, catching an icy-cold mouthful as she hit the deck. She heard him pause behind, breathing laboured, and hauled herself up.

"Isla, don't," he called, as she set off running again.

She knew it was futile. He was almost upon her.

"Isla." The gruff way he shouted made her shudder as his arm snaked around her neck.

He dragged her towards the tree line, her feet fighting desperately for a grip as she attempted to free herself. In the distance, sirens approached. They strengthened her resolve to fight back, and she clawed at the GP, nails scraping at his face. Icy air burned her lungs as panic blurred her vision.

"Let go of me!" She forced the words past his hand, her voice hoarse and raw.

"Stop struggling!" he barked back, breath hot against her ear. She could hear the strain in his voice, and a desperation amidst the anger.

The designer thrashed harder, twisting her body to jab an elbow backward into his ribs.

He grunted, loosening his hold enough for her to stagger free.

She stumbled sideways, clutching her throat, gasping for air.

The approaching sirens squealed through the deepening night, reverberating through the park. She saw flashes of blue reflecting off snow-laden trees. Hope surged in her chest.

MacNeil lunged, grabbing her wrist with a force that made her scream. "You've left me no choice," he hissed, pulling her toward a dense cluster of trees. "I didn't want it to come to this."

"Like hell you didn't," she spat, digging her heels into the snow, gouging muddy lines through the white blanket, but he was far stronger than she.

A low growl broke through the din of sirens. Isla's head snapped toward the sound just as a police dog and its handler emerged running along the path ahead. The dog barked fiercely, straining against its lead.

"Police! Let her go!" the officer bellowed as he loosed the dog from its leash.

MacNeil froze.

Isla seized the moment, twisting violently away from him. She fell hard onto the snowy ground, curling into a ball to protect herself from the snarling dog fast approaching.

She needn't have worried. The dog ignored her. Instead, it tore after her attacker as the doctor made off in the opposite direction.

"Don't even think about it, MacNeil!" A voice boomed from among the approaching officers. Isla recognised that voice. DI McKenzie.

MacNeil didn't hear him. He was too busy trying to fight off teeth, claws, and fur as the determined canine took him down.

Susan Robertson pulled the shaking and breathless Isla to safety, guiding her away while wrapping a yellow police-issue jacket over her trembling frame. The designer turned her gaze to MacNeil as two officers moved in to cuff him. She turned away, tears rolling down her face. She couldn't watch anymore.

19

SHAKEN, NOT STIRRED

The office was alive with the chatter of MIT officers and the few uniformed colleagues who had joined them as they celebrated catching their killer. A box of pastries sat on the corner of McKenzie's desk, already half-empty, while a teapot, cups, and a carton of milk stood clustered together like old friends.

Susan Robertson poured herself a mug as the late afternoon sun streamed through the window, catching the steam as it curled upward from their drinks.

"Thanks, everyone." McKenzie leaned back in his chair, hands behind his head. "I have to say I was terrified we wouldn't get to Isla Campbell in time."

Susan grinned, plucking crumbs from her sleeve. "The look of shock on MacNeil's face was priceless when he saw the dogs. He's probably never run so fast in his life."

Dalgleish swallowed a mouthful of cake, washing it down with tea. "Aye, so much for the Hippocratic oath, eh?"

Grant nodded. "That man was ruthless, murdering not only his wife while she was still at college, but anyone else that might expose him."

"Aye," McAllister agreed, "and sending threatening letters to himself and the rest of the friends so he could get away with murdering Caitlin, the only serious threat to his freedom because she knew what he had done."

"But I don't understand why he killed her when he did." Graham frowned. "I mean, if she was going to expose him, surely she would have done it years before?"

The DI sat upright. "I agree. He must have trusted her not to say anything early on. Something must have changed. Or perhaps she said something to him that got him worried. It was his aftershave I smelled in her wardrobe. And Isla gave us this..." He held up the photograph of the oak tree given to the designer by Caitlin. "It's the oak near Tring station. She thinks Caitlin kept the photo because she believed Miranda to be buried underneath it. And it was only her lifelong friendship with MacNeil that stopped her from telling police what she knew years ago. It must have weighed heavily on her before her death."

"And maybe she finally said something to MacNeil... Told him to come clean," Susan said.

"Aye, but MacNeil is staying tight-lipped. He's not admitting anything. But the Met are seeking permission to excavate the hill under the oak. This morning they saw anomalies with ground-penetrating radar, and think they have found where she may be buried."

"Let's hope it is Miranda. Her family can have closure after all these years."

"Well done, you lot." DCI Sinclair poked his head around the door. "Have you saved any of that cake for me?"

"No." McKenzie grinned.

"Och, away with you, ya bugger." Rob grabbed a pastry. "Seriously, I think Ms Campbell is lucky to be alive."

"She gave him a run for his money. Jeezo." Grant

nodded. "That's one brave lady. But I suspect the others never saw it coming. MacNeil is a coward. He lay in wait for his first victims. He probably used the same method to take out his wife."

"Well, a dangerous man is off the streets, and justice has been served. That's what this job is about." The DCI picked up a mug, pouring himself some tea. "Though I don't know what his surgery is going to do. I guess they'll need a locum for the interim."

"To the team." Dalgleish raised his mug.

"To the team," the rest echoed, raising theirs.

"So, what's next?" Susan asked.

"Sleep," Grant suggested. "But there's still a part of the puzzle I haven't worked out."

"What's that?" Graham cocked his head.

"That black Lexus. We never found out who it belonged to. It's not MacNeil's car."

DCI Sinclair cleared his throat. "Ah... I can help with that," he said.

"Can you?" McKenzie's brow furrowed.

"Uh huh... We weren't the only ones investigating Caitlin's death."

Realisation dawned, and the DI could have kicked himself. "Spooks?" he asked.

Rob nodded. "I cannot elaborate more than that, I'm afraid."

"And we beat them to it?" Grant shook his head. "Now that, I find hard to believe."

"Maybe they had their heads elsewhere, thinking it was gang revenge. But I don't think they'd have been far behind."

Susan perched on the end of a desk. "To be fair, they may have gotten to the answer before us, actually. But because it didn't relate to Caitlin's undercover work, they left us to do our job."

McKenzie nodded. "In a way, Caitlin helped us too, with that photo she kept of the oak tree. It was her insurance in the event Douglas went after her."

"To Caitlin Murray." Helen raised her mug.

"To Caitlin," the rest concurred.

∽

THE END.

AFTERWORD

Watch out for Book 5 in the DI McKenzie Series, coming soon...

Mailing list: You can join my emailing list here : AnnamarieMorgan.com

Facebook page: AnnamarieMorganAuthor

Book 1: Murder on Arthur's Seat

When DI Grant McKenzie's world is thrown into chaos by the sudden disappearance of his twenty-one-year-old nephew, he is determined to uncover the truth no matter the cost.

As he and his team are plunged into a dark and sinister web of organised crime, McKenzie must face a wealthy and elusive kingpin who believes himself untouchable. With the fate of his nephew hanging in the balance, McKenzie and his team will stop at nothing to bring the criminal mastermind to justice.

Book 2: Murder at Greyfriars Kirk

When a young influencer is found dead in an Edinburgh

graveyard, the contents of her last video provide an enigmatic, if not downright cryptic, insight into the woman's last moments.

DI Grant McKenzie cannot shake the feeling the woman was trying to communicate more than a historical tale for her followers. Did she know what was about to happen?

As more influencers fall prey to the same killer, the DI and his team face a heart-stopping race to find an evil psychopath who sneaks up on preoccupied prey; the man the press has named The Gimbal Killer.

Book 3: Murder in the Bookkeeper's Attic

When an elderly book lover is murdered in an attic full of books, DI Grant McKenzie and his team are baffled regarding the motive. Everybody insists they loved the man and would never wish him harm. The only clue may lie in the bookkeeper's last social media post in which he stated he had in his possession the 'Whitlock Tome', a book said to have been written during the First World War, that disappeared during the 1920s and is rumoured to have encoded within it the whereabouts of a valuable family heirloom or secret.

DI McKenzie knows only one thing for sure: the book if it exists, is missing. And those who previously possessed it are dead. Who killed the bookkeeper? Where is the Whitlock Tome? And could anyone else fall victim to the same madman who murdered the avid collector? As the stakes climb ever higher, DI McKenzie and his team pull out all the stops to catch a mysterious and ruthless killer before he strikes again.

You might also like to read the author's other books.
The DI Giles Series:

Book 1: Death Master:

After months of mental and physical therapy, Yvonne Giles, an Oxford DI, is back at work and that's just how she likes it. So when she's asked to hunt the serial killer responsible for taking apart young women, the DI jumps at the chance but hides the fact she is suffering debilitating flashbacks. She is told to work with Tasha Phillips, an in-her-face, criminal psychologist. The DI is not enamoured with the idea. Tasha has a lot to prove. Yvonne has a lot to get over. A tentative link with a 20 year-old cold case brings them closer to the truth but events then take a horrifyingly personal turn.

Book 2: You Will Die

After apprehending an Oxford Serial Killer, and almost losing her life in the process, DI Yvonne Giles has left England for a quieter life in rural Wales. Her peace is shattered when she is asked to hunt a priest-killing psychopath, who taunts the police with messages inscribed on the corpses. Yvonne requests the help of Dr. Tasha Phillips, a psychologist and friend, to aid in the hunt. But the killer is one step ahead and the ultimatum, he sets them, could leave everyone devastated.

Book 3: Total Wipeout

A whole family is wiped out with a shotgun. At first glance, it's an open-and-shut case. The dad did it, then killed himself. The deaths follow at least two similar family wipeouts – attributed to the financial crash.

So why doesn't that sit right with Detective Inspector Yvonne Giles? And why has a rape occurred in the area, in the weeks preceding each family's demise? Her seniors do not believe there are questions to answer. DI Giles must therefore risk everything, in a high-stakes investigation ofa mysterious masonic ring and players in high finance.

Can she find the answers, before the next innocent family is wiped out?

Book 4: Deep Cut
In a tiny hamlet in North Wales, a female recruit is murdered whilst on Christmas home leave. Detective Inspector Yvonne Giles is asked to cut short her own leave, to investigate. Why was the young soldier killed? And is her death related to several alleged suicides at her army base? DI Giles this it is, and that someone powerful has a dark secret they will do anything to hide.

Book 5: The Pusher
Young men are turning up dead on the banks of the River Severn. Some of them have been missing for days or even weeks. The only thing the police can be sure of, is that the men have drowned. Rumours abound that a mythical serial killer has turned his attention from the Manchester canal to the waterways of Mid-Wales. And now one of CID's own is missing. A brand new recruit with everything to live for. DI Giles must find him before it's too late.

Book 6: Gone
Children are going missing. They are not heard from again until sinister requests for cryptocurrency go viral. The public must pay or the children die. For lead detective Yvonne Giles, the case is complicated enough. And then the unthinkable happens...

Book 7: Bone Dancer
A serial killer is murdering women, threading their

bones back together, and leaving them for police to find. Detective Inspector Yvonne Giles must find him before more innocent victims die. Problem is, the killer wants her and will do anything he can to get her. Unaware that she, herself, is is a target, DI Giles risks everything to catch him.

Book 8: Blood Lost

A young man comes home to find his whole family missing. Half-eaten breakfasts and blood spatter on the lounge wall are the only clues to what happened...

Book 9: Angel of Death

The peace of the Mid-Wales countryside is shattered, when a female eco-warrior is found crucified in a public wood. At first, it would appear a simple case of finding which of the woman's enemies had had her killed. But DI Yvonne Giles has no idea how bad things are going to get. As the body count rises, she will need all of her instincts, and the skills of those closest to her, to stop the murderous rampage of the Angel of Death.

Book 10: Death in the Air

Several fatal air collisions have occurred within a few months in rural Wales. According to the local Air Accidents Investigation Branch (AAIB) inspector, it's a coincidence. Clusters happen. Except, this cluster is different. DI Yvonne Giles suspects it when she hears some of the witness statements but, when an AAIB inspector is found dead under a bridge, she knows it.

Something is way off. Yvonne is determined to get to the bottom of the mystery, but exactly how far down the treacherous rabbit hole is she prepared to go?

Book 11: Death in the Mist

The morning after a viscous sea-mist covers the seaside town of Aberystwyth, a young student lies brutalised within one hundred yards of the castle ruins.

DI Yvonne Giles' reputation precedes her. Having successfully captured more serial killers than some detectives have caught colds, she is seconded to head the murder investigation team, and hunt down the young woman's killer.

What she doesn't know, is this is only the beginning...

Book 12: Death under Hypnosis

When the secretive and mysterious Sheila Winters approaches Yvonne Giles and tells her that she murdered someone thirty years before, she has the DI's immediate attention.

Things get even more strange when Sheila states:
She doesn't know who.
She doesn't know where.
She doesn't know why.

Book 13: Fatal Turn

A seasoned hiker goes missing from the Dolfor Moors after recording a social media video describing a narrow cave he intends to explore. A tragic accident? Nothing to see here, until a team of cavers disappear on a coastal potholing expedition, setting off a string of events that has DI Giles tearing her hair out. What, or who is the thread that ties this series of disappearances together?

A serial killer, thriller murder-mystery set in Wales.

Book 14: The Edinburgh Murders

A newly-retired detective from the Met is murdered in a

murky alley in Edinburgh, a sinister calling card left with the body.

The dead man had been a close friend of psychologist Tasha Phillips, giving her her first gig with the Met decades before.

Tasha begs DI Yvonne Giles to aid the Scottish police in solving the case.

In unfamiliar territory, and with a ruthless killer haunting the streets, the DI plunges herself into one of the darkest, most terrifying cases of her career. Who exactly is The Poet?

Book 15: A Picture of Murder

Men are being thrown to their deaths in rural Wales.

At first glance, the murders appear unconnected until DI Giles uncovers potential links with a cold case from the turn of the Millennium.

Someone is eliminating the witnesses to a double murder.

DI Giles and her team must find the perpetrator before all the witnesses are dead.

Book 16: The Wilderness Murders

People are disappearing from remote locations.

Abandoned cars, neatly piled belongings, and bizarre last photographs, are the only clues for what happened to them.

Did they run away? Or, as DI Giles suspects, have they fallen prey to a serial killer who is taunting police with the heinous pieces of a puzzle they must solve if they are to stop the wilderness murderer.

Book 17: The Bunker Murders

A murder victim found in a shallow grave has DI Yvonne Giles and her team on the hunt for both the killer and a motive for the well-loved man's demise.

Yvonne cannot help feeling the killing is linked to a string of female disappearances stretching back nearly two decades.

Someone has all the answers, and the DI will stop at nothing to find them and get to the bottom of this perplexing mystery.

Book 18: The Garthmyl Murders

A missing brother and friends with dark secrets have DI Giles turning circles after a body is found face-down in the pond of a local landmark.

Stymied by a wall of silence and superstition, Yvonne and her team must dig deeper than ever if they are to crack this impossible case.

Who, or what, is responsible for the Garthmyl murders?

Book 19: The Signature

When a young woman is found dead inside a rubbish dumpster after a night out, police chiefs are quick to label it a tragic accident. But as more bodies surface, Detective Inspector Yvonne Giles is convinced a cold-blooded murderer is on the loose. She believes the perpetrator is devious and elusive, disabling CCTV cameras in the area, and leaving them with little to go on. With time running out, Giles and her team must race against the clock to catch the killer or killers before they strike again.

Book 20: The Incendiary Murders

When the Powys mansion belonging to an ageing rock star is rocked by a deadly explosion, Detective Inspector

Yvonne Giles finds herself tasked with a case of murder, suspicion, and secrets. As shockwaves ripple through the community, Giles must pierce the impenetrable facades of the characters surrounding the case, racing the clock to find the culprit and prevent further bombings. With an investigation full of twists and turns, DI Yvonne Giles must unravel the truth before it's too late.

Book 21 - The Park Murders

When two people are left dead and four others are seriously ill in hospital after a visit to a local nature park in rural Wales, DI Giles and her team find themselves in a race against time to stop a killer or killers hell-bent on terrorising the community. As the investigation deepens, the team must draw on all of their skill and experience to hunt down the elusive Powys poisoner before more lives are lost.

Book 22 - The Powys Murders

Three bodies are discovered in a wood when snow and ice melt from the Powys countryside. Police suspect the dead men were involved in a road traffic collision before they ran off into the darkness and succumbed to exposure.

What made them run uphill into the wilderness instead of downhill to the nearest town? Were all of their injuries inflicted by the collision? Or something more sinister? And why was one victim missing his shoes?

DI Yvonne Giles suspects foul play, believing the men ran the wrong way because they were terrified. Who, or what, was responsible for the deaths of The Powys Three? And are others at risk from the same evil?

Book 23: The Backstreet Murders

Murder and mystery collide on the dark streets of Newtown when a body is unceremoniously thrown from a car in the dead of night. DI Yvonne Giles and her team are thrust into a high-stakes hunt for the killer and the truth behind the victim's tragic demise. But as they dig deeper, they uncover a tangled web of secrets and lies that hide the keys to solving the case. And when they discover that the victim's best friend vanished without a trace seventeen years ago, the mystery only deepens. Who killed the man on the tarmac? And what really happened to his best friend? With time running out and a potential witness gone missing, DI Giles must race against the clock to crack the case and bring the killer to justice before it's too late.

Remember to watch out for Book 24 in the DI Giles Series, coming soon...

Printed in Great Britain
by Amazon